LIQUID DEATH

A gang of criminals has established a far reaching racket in counterfeit coins, making English gold sovereigns to order. The CID is kept busy, but then there's a mysterious epidemic of deaths from snakebites. Chief Inspector Dawson of the Metropolitan Division's scientific branch discovers the relationship between deadly snakebite and counterfeit coins. Dawson is aided by Detective-Sergeant Harriday and Gwenda Blane. But Dawson and his colleagues risk their lives attempting to smash a ruthless homicidal racket . . .

JOHN RUSSELL FEARN

LIQUID DEATH

Complete and Unabridged

LINFORD
Leicester

First published in Great Britain

First Linford Edition
published 2009

British Library CIP Data

Fearn, John Russell, *1908 – 1960.*
  Liquid death- - (Linford mystery library)
  1. Counterfeits and counterfeiting- -Fiction.
  2. Detective and mystery stories.
  3. Large type books.
  I. Title II. Series
  823.9'12–dc22

ISBN 978–1–84782–826–2

Published by
F. A. Thorpe (Publishing)
Anstey, Leicestershire

Set by Words & Graphics Ltd.
Anstey, Leicestershire
Printed and bound in Great Britain by
T. J. International Ltd., Padstow, Cornwall

This book is printed on acid-free paper

1

The man in the cloth cap, coarse flannel shirt, and corduroy trousers tied just below the knee with string was obviously a labourer. For this very reason he looked distinctly incongruous as he waited outside the polished green door of a typical London house of the Georgian period. After his ringing at the bell there was a long interval, then the door opened and a manservant gazed out into the late summer afternoon in obvious horror.

'Tradesmen's entrance is at the rear,' he stated briefly. 'On your way, my man.'

'I would if I wus a tradesman — but I'm not.' The man gave a broad grin. 'Nick Gregson's the name, pal. I want to see the guv'nor.'

'You cannot possibly mean . . . '

'I mean Henry Garside, the bloke as owns them 'ouses down Stepney way. The ones that's bein' demolished now.'

The manservant frowned and then

1

seemed to recollect something. 'Am I to understand you are connected with the demolition firm, Mr. — er — Gregson?'

'Right, pal. And I must see the guv. It's important.'

The manservant's nostrils distended. 'I will enquire if the master is at home. Wait there.'

The labourer shrugged and took a firmer hold of the stiff brown paper parcel he was hugging. Or rather, it was dirty yellow, splashed with whitewash, and advertised a famous cement. Plainly it had been picked up on the demolition site.

'This way,' the manservant directed coldly reappearing. 'And wipe those boots, if you don't mind.'

Nick Gregson humbly did as ordered and then took off his cap from lank hair as he followed the majestic being across a sombre, spotless hall to a nearby door. Once beyond it, Nick found himself facing a tubby, middle-aged man in a velvet smoking jacket, reclining in a deep armchair beside the fire. Having evidently been forewarned as to the appearance of his visitor, he expressed no surprise as he viewed him.

'Well, my man? And what can I do for you? Excuse my not asking you to sit down. Those working clothes are hardly . . .'

'Aw, that's all right, guv'nor. This won't take long.'

Gregson brought the dirty paper bag more clearly into view and was about to dump it on the Shereton occasional table when a howl of protest stopped him.

'Not on your life, man! Don't you dare dump anything on that table! Come to the point, can't you?'

'All right. See this bag? In it there's five hundred sovereigns! Queen Victoria, from the look of 'em.'

'Why come to me?' Henry Garside's pink face was impatient.

'Because I thought as 'ow you might like to buy 'em. Nice price for sovereigns these days, guv'nor. Around forty-five quid a sov., isn't it?'

'I'm not certain of the exact market value. And I repeat — why come to me? Why don't you take them to a pawn-broker, or somebody?'

'Because a bloke like me might get looked at, with five 'undred sovereigns! 'Sides, there's a reason why I've come to you. I found these this afternoon in an old tin box in number six, Fordney Crescent, one of them rows of 'ouses of yours which we're wreckin'. I s'pose I should've let the foreman know about it, but instead, I got to thinkin'. I found 'em, and there's some sort of law about buried treasure that lets a man keep what he finds — or a part of it, or summat.'

Garside's impatience had gone. He was looking astonished instead. After thinking for a moment he took up a newspaper from the stand beside him and spread it over his immaculate trousers.

'Come over here, my man. Let me see some of those coins.'

Nick Gregson moved swiftly and, from the cement bag, poured about a score of the old, stained coins on to the newspaper. Garside picked several of them up in turn, examined them intently, and finally began to nod his bald head slowly back and forth.

'Mmm, seems little doubt about it, my

man. So you found them in number six, Fordney Crescent, did you? Whereabouts?'

'Under the ground floor — but I kept it to meself.'

'Very illegal of you — but I'm damned if I blame you for that! Let me see, now; my tenant at number six was — ' Garside mused with his mouth open. 'Oh, yes, Mrs. Brice. The little widow with hardly a penny to her name. Dead now, though. No guarantee the sovereigns were hers, anyway. So you came to hand them over to me? That was very honest of you, Mr. Gregson. To be strictly accurate, the police should be told.'

The labourer's expression changed. 'Now, wait a minute, guv. I didn't come to give 'em to you. I want to sell 'em. More chance of doing it to you than to a pop-shop. Somebody might try an' say I pinched 'em. Five hundred sovs. take a lot of explaining.'

'On my property, Mr. Gregson — therefore I call them mine.'

'Findings keepings, I say.'

'No doubt . . . ' Garside's face melted

slowly into a grin. 'However, I'm not a hard man and you are obviously far more in need of money than I am. I'll buy them from you — at twenty-two pounds fifty a sovereign.'

Gregson glared. 'What in hell sort uv a bargain is that? These is worth forty-five pounds each — or near it.'

'Exactly. Hence the fifty-fifty. You hardly expect me to pay market value, do you? What would I get out of it?'

'Same's you've paid me! Fair's fair, I say.'

The smile on Garside's cherubic faded again. 'Better take my offer, Mr. Gregson. If I withdraw it, I can claim all these, and you'll get nothing. You seem good at sayings; you would do well to remember one about looking a gift horse in the mouth.'

Gregson scowled in thought and rubbed the back of his weather-beaten neck. Then, at last, he sighed.

'Okay — I'll take it. I'll probably get nothing the other way. Let's see — that's twenty-two pounds fifty, five hundred times, and . . . ' he broke off, floundering.

'Eleven thousand, two hundred and fifty pounds, my man, and consider yourself well paid. Let me see them all. Here — put them on the rug.'

Garside spread the newspaper at his feet and emptied the dirty bag over it. For the next twenty minutes Garside was busy counting and re-counting, then at last he struggled from his knees to his feet and lumbered across to a wall safe.

'Naturally, you'll prefer cash?' he asked over his shoulder.

'I ain't got no blasted bank account, if that's what you mean.'

'Quite so.' From the safe Garside took the required amount in high denomination notes and handed them over. Gregson went through them steadily with a dirty thumb and forefinger, and finally he nodded.

'Thanks, guv. Not what I expected, but it'll have to do.'

'And should you find any more sovereigns on my property in the course of its demolishing, we can perhaps do further business, my friend. Good day to you.'

Gregson nodded and took his departure at the side of the scandalized manservant — and it was about this time that a similar scene to the Gregson-Garside performance was being enacted in the Soho district, and this time, the setting was Reuben Goldstein's, the pawnbroker.

Reuben Goldstein was no longer a young man.

His eyes had no longer their intense keenness. He did not hear so well any more, either — but there was not much he missed. And he watched with interest as two customers arrived together almost at closing time. One was a man of apparent age — early eighties at least — and with him was a powerful young man who proudly carried a wooden box on one broad shoulder. Plainly it was heavy, for he dropped it with considerable force on the counter and then mopped his sharp-featured face.

'Good evening, gentlemen.' Goldstein looked from one to the other and rubbed his gnarled hands together.

'And vot is your pleasure?'

The elderly man, impeccably dressed, raised his malacca cane briefly. 'Open it up, Harry. Let him see.'

'Okay, grandpa.' The young man pulled a small screwdriver from his pocket, removed three screws from the box's wooden lid, then heaved it up on hinges. The pawnbroker gazed fixedly, much as Edmond Dantes must have done when he first beheld the treasure of Monte Cristo

'Sovereigns!' he exclaimed, throwing up his hands. 'I never saw so many sovereigns all at vun time!'

'Mr. Goldstein, there are five thousand sovereigns there!' The elderly man spoke with firm, cultured quietness. 'The collection of a lifetime. I am eighty-six years of age, and have spent my life collecting sovereigns as a hobby. Now I know I have not much longer to go, I am selling my possessions, and that naturally includes these. I assume you are interested? My grandson here remarked that you are one of the fairest dealers in this region.'

'I always give a square deal!' Goldstein looked very resolute about it, his hooked nose nearly touching his chin. 'But five t'ousand! That is a lot of gold.'

'Course it is! I wouldn't be wasting my time on trifles, believe me. It isn't money I need; just commonsense value for my offspring. Take them — take them. Look at them. Test them.'

Goldstein scooped up a handful of the coins and disappeared to mysterious regions at the shop's rear. The young man and the elderly man exchanged glances and waited. Then, at length, Goldstein came back.

'Obviously, I cannot take time to count five t'ousand coins, so I . . . '

'There are five thousand, Mr. Goldstein. You have my word on that. And, let me tell you, it has never been broken.'

'I vould not doubt it for a moment — not for a moment. And I vould like to do business. These sovereigns I have tested are perfect — real gold.'

The elderly man looked indignant. 'Did you think they were brass?'

'I am a business man,' Goldstein said solemnly. 'I have to weigh gold and test it with acid. If those two tests are right, then

I am glad. But to count and test five t'ousand of them is a long job. Ve can do business,' he finished firmly, 'if you trust me with these sovereigns until this time tomorrow night.'

The elderly man reflected, then the young man gave a shrug.

'Might as well, grandpa. Whoever you take these coins to, they'd have to examine them as Mr. Goldstein wishes to do. Only to be expected.'

'Ah, well — I suppose so. I so dislike delays. Very well, Mr. Goldstein; give me your receipt and I will return this time tomorrow. My name is Vincent P. Caxton — if you wish to know.'

Goldstein nodded and laboriously wrote out a receipt, upon which his two customers left with the promise to return at five-forty-five the following afternoon.

And, at the home of a certain famous financier and industrialist in Mayfair, there took place that same evening a most confidential meeting between the financier himself — Elliot K. Marsden — and the globe-trotter Jeremiah (Jerry) Bax.

Jerry was just back from a jaunt that

had kept him out of England for twelve years.

Long enough for society to forget about him, even to think of him as a complete stranger when he landed back. Jerry Bax was a clever man. He had the charm necessary to convince the devil himself that black can be white — sometimes.

'Thirty thousand sovereigns, eh?' Elliot K. Marsden drew gently on his cigar and surveyed the three boxes which three strong servants had carried into this library a little while earlier. 'It's mighty good going, Jerry.'

'So I think.' Jerry was a tall, easy-going man in the early fifties, military in features, bronzed in complexion, and nearly always smiling. 'I never expected to find the damned treasure mind you. I knew of it from an old sailor friend of mine. He knew the stuff had been buried on one of the remote Pacific islands when the ship carrying it had been wrecked, but I was the only man to find it. Naturally, I want to make something out of it. It occurred to me you might want to make something out of it, too — not as actual sovereigns, but as gold in bulk. So it's up to you.'

The financier picked up one or two of the coins and examined them intently.

'They look genuine enough.'

'Look! They damned well are. Put them through any test you like.'

'I intend to, before we talk business. I've asked Walters to come over. He's my chief analyst.'

'Analyst?' Jerry frowned. 'What on earth has a financier in common with an analyst?'

Elliot K. grinned. 'You've evidently forgotten that I own a number of combines — steel, rubber, plastics, and heaven knows what. I could be swindled with materials if it were not for my analysts — and Walters is the best of them all.'

Jerry shrugged. 'Okay. But I'm surprised you can't take my word. I'm well known enough.'

'With all due respect, Jerry, I've only your word for that, too. Nobody seems to remember you in select circles, in spite of your saying you were once closely connected with them.'

'Twelve years is a long time, E.K. People forget, and . . . '

'Mr. Walters, sir,' the manservant announced gravely as he appeared like a phantom.

'Oh, yes, Peters; show him in here, please.'

Walters was a thin-nosed, unsmiling man of uncertain age, carrying with him a square box of portable equipment. He said 'good evening' to his employer, nodded briefly to Jerry Bax and then — having been given his instructions beforehand — went to work on six selected sovereigns. In silence the industrialist and the explorer watched him, even though they could not follow the entire sequence of the test. The acid and the weight tests were obvious enough, but other experiments between magnets, and using instruments like flashlamps except that they had no beams — were beyond them. Nor did Walters' expression give anything away.

Finally, however, he folded up his equipment and tossed the coins back in the nearest box.

'Genuine gold in each case, Mr. Marsden,' he announced. 'Atomic weight is correct, and so is the response to ultrasonic vibration. Acid-proof and correct normal weight — as opposed to atomic.'

'Then, if those six are pure gold, so must the others be?'

Walters flashed a brief glance at Jerry. 'I suppose so. One could hardly select six at random, sir, and have all the others spurious.'

'I should damned well think not!' Jerry objected. 'Look here, E.K., what do you take me for?'

'All right — no offence!' the financier grinned. 'Can't blame me for taking precautions. Right, Walters, that's all. Many thanks.'

The analyst nodded and took his departure. Marsden poured out drinks and brought them back to the table, handing one to Jerry.

'All right — we talk business,' he said. 'What's your price?'

'Top market value, of course. Two hundred and twenty-five thousand pounds. I can get that anywhere, and you know it. You, using them for their actual gold value, can probably make a handsome profit, even at that figure.'

'Could be,' the tycoon grinned. 'But my figure is one hundred and ninety thousand, top limit. I'm going to be under considerable expense operating with so much gold.'

'One hundred and ninety-five thousand, or I go elsewhere.'

Marsden reflected and then held out his hand. 'One hundred and ninety-five thousand it is. You shall have my cheque before you leave this evening. Now let's have another drink.'

★　★　★

A week after the various negotiations in sovereigns had been completed, a group of men sat in a secluded country house some thirty miles from London. The house was unique in that it stood in its own somewhat neglected grounds and that the nearest neighbour was a good three miles away. Even the main road that ran from London to the south coast was a good half-mile distant so, in every way, the house was admirably suited for men working against the law.

The men arrived at the house by different routes and at varying intervals, and always by night. Unless they were specially watched, which they were quite certain they were not, nobody could report upon their comings and goings. So, finally, every man was present. Two of them were the elderly gentleman of culture and his powerful 'grandson'; another was Nick Gregson from the demolition squad; and there was also the smiling, military looking Jerry Bax. In addition to these, there also lounged in the big, comfortably furnished library a square-headed, unimaginative strong-arm man by the name of 'Mopes' McCall, two years a fugitive from Dartmoor, and of whom the police had lost trace.

They waited without speaking to each other, some of them smoking and meditating, others playing cards. But each was alert for the least sound from the night outside. It was nearly midnight, and

17

one more had still to come.

He came just after Jerry Bax had glanced at his watch — and immediately every man was on his feet, revolver or automatic ready for action, only to replace them as the immaculate man known only as the 'Chief' came into the library. All knew his real identity and his position in the social scale, but none had ever dared to betray him. He was much too powerful for that.

'Good evening, gentlemen,' he said briefly, removing his overcoat, homburg and scarf. 'All of you here, I see. Good! I only hope the presence of each one of you is indicative of good news.'

'Far as I'm concerned, Chief, no doubt about it,' Jerry Bax remarked, lighting a cigarette.

'Splendid!' The Chief crossed to the deep armchair beside the electric fire and settled himself. 'Now, my friends, how is the little business with the sovereigns progressing? Your reports, please, one at a time. You first, Jerry.'

Jerry grinned and, from his wallet, handed across Elliot K. Marsden's open checque for £195,000. The Chief took it and raised his eyebrows.

'I said two hundred and twenty-five thousand, Jerry. What's this?'

'Best I could do. Marsden's no easy nut to crack. You know as well as I do that that many sovereigns couldn't be handled — er — conveniently in the ordinary course of business, except over a very long period. I took the best bargain I could.'

'Mmm. Very well. And you, Larry?'

The elderly culturist smiled complacently and produced another check.

'Twenty two thousand five hundred, Chief. Full market price, and not much trouble, either. Goldstein was extremely thorough before he'd part with his money, though.'

The Chief smiled.

'My congratulations, Larry — and to your mythical grandson. And what about you, Nick?'

Nick Gregson looked uncomfortable as he handed over a large envelope containing his £11,250. The Chief counted the notes swiftly and then narrowed his eyes.

'Where's the rest of it, Nick?'

'That's all there is, Chief — so help me! That old devil Garside beat me down to half price — an' even less — an' there wus nothin' I could do about it. I said at first that idea of plantin' me an' them sovereigns in a demolition area wus crazy; now I'm sure of it.'

'I placed you, Nick, where your lack of education and finesse fitted you best. You've done very badly, but I'm prepared to believe you are speaking the truth, because you know where you'll finish up if you are not . . .'

The Chief made a mental calculation. 'Two hundred and twenty eight thousand, seven hundred and fifty pounds. Very fair, considering our actual outlay has not been very great. Fifty per cent of this total is mine, and the remainder is yours to divide between you as you see fit. I'll have no part in your squabbles as you endeavor to apportion it. Understand?'

The others nodded silently and looked menacingly at each other — or, more correctly, Nick Gregson looked menacingly at everybody else.

'What about me, Chief?' 'Mopes' McCall objected, his chair on its hind legs against the wall. 'Don't I get anythin' for stayin' here like a dumb cluck in case anything happens?'

'You get your normal pay, 'Mopes', and nothing else. You can't be expected to cash in on proceeds which you haven't attempted to earn.'

'I was willin'!' 'Mopes' shouted, pulling an immensely thick notebook from his shirt pocket. 'Look here, I've a list of mugs who'd fall for the sovereign racket any time we . . . '

'I'll decide how to run our — er — financial concern,' the Chief interrupted. 'Don't start getting big ideas, 'Mopes', in case the police suddenly discover where you are.'

Muttering to himself, 'Mopes' relaxed again, inspecting his thick notebook pensively, then Jerry Bax asked a question somewhat uncertainly:

'When these sovereigns reach the markets, Chief, isn't there likely to be trouble?'

'Why should there be? Sovereigns are

being found every day by all manner of people. A sudden influx of them should not occasion any surprise. Even if it does, it doesn't matter. These sovereigns are real gold, even though they have never been actually in the Royal Mint at any time.'

Jerry shook his head worriedly. 'That's the bit I can't get over — how you produce real gold without there being any. It's nothin' short of damned uncanny!'

The Chief shrugged. 'One might as well say that it is uncanny for somebody's moving picture to be projected for thousands of miles through empty space — but it isn't. We call it television. It is simply an accomplishment of science — just as is the art of turning base metals and unwanted alloys into gold. We live in a scientific age, my friend, and the old days of the counterfeiter, with his clumsy press, have gone into the discard, along with the horse-drawn trams. I must admit, though,' the Chief added pensively, 'that I hit on the secret by accident. When I knew I could manufacture gold whenever I wanted, the thing to do was to distribute it. Hence my selection of each one of you. Just the right type! All of you wanted by the law. One word from me, and . . . '

There was silence for a moment. Then another blunt question — this time from the 'grandson'.

'If you can make gold as easily as you say you can, why all this messing about with sovereigns and making the right contacts to receive them? Why don't you cut everybody else out, make gold bricks, and dump them in your bank?'

'You reveal profound lack of experience, my young friend,' the Chief commented. 'One cannot haphazardly dump gold bricks in a bank, as you seem to think. A strict watch is kept on all gold reserves, and one or several gold bricks out of thin air would be a matter for investigation. Sovereigns, though, can appear in their thousands without raising suspicion, being deemed the secret hordes of misers, financiers, and such. It is by far the best method. Slow, yes — but sure. For instance, having just completed a clean-up, we must now lie low for a time.'

'For myself, sir,' observed Larry, the elderly man, 'I bow before your scientific knowledge. We have a brilliant man leading us — brilliant in crime and in his normal profession.'

'We'll keep my normal profession out of this,' the Chief said brusquely. 'And to satisfy all of you, now I know you are to be trusted — otherwise you would have tried to give me the slip with much of the money you've recently made — I'll show you just what is done to make these coins. 'Mopes' knows already, since he guards this place but, fortunately, he hasn't the intelligence to understand anything.'

The gunman's thick lips opened at the start of a protest, and then closed again. Scowling, he resumed his study of the thick notebook he still held in his beefy hands.

The Chief rose. 'Come with me, my friends. I think you will be intrigued — with the possible exception of Nick here, whose mentality is about on a par with that of 'Mopes'.'

'At least I can pull a deal, which is

more'n he can do!' Nick objected.

'Pull a deal? At half the possible value? My dear Nick!'

Smiling cynically, the Chief opened the library door and led the way across the broad hall. Presently he reached the panelled side of the massive staircase, one of which panels flew open under the actuation of a tiny switch. Beyond the panel loomed a staircase, clearly illuminated since lights from below had automatically come into action.

'You know, my friends,' the Chief commented, as he led the way downstairs, 'I count myself lucky to have been able to buy this old mansion. Absolutely ideal in every way — even to these great wine cellars that I have turned into one big laboratory. Ah, here we are. Look around for yourselves.'

The assembled men were already doing so, mostly in amazement. Nick Gregson indeed was pretty near to gaping and perhaps with good reason. There was electrical apparatus in all directions, and practically all of it of highly modern electronic design. There were also anode and cathode globes on pillars, electro-magnets, cathode ray tubes, and all manner of complicated equipment of like character.

'You must use plenty of juice to run this laboratory, Chief,' Jerry Bax commented. 'Aren't you afraid the power and light authorities might ask questions some time?'

'There's your answer to that.' The Chief indicated three massive generators. 'I use enough power to start them up and, after that, they run themselves in non-stop stages and, of course, they supply me with adequate power. Yes, my friends, there is a wealth of secrets down here; the accumulation of years of specialized knowledge — to say nothing of the expenditure of a considerable amount of money. And if you have scientific knowledge, you might as well use it to the best advantage. Government scientists, one of which I could have become — are poorly paid. I prefer big money, and in time I shall have it. All of us will.'

There was a pause as the men surveyed

the other part of the laboratory, which appeared to be devoted to chemistry, judging from the test-tubes, retorts and scores of mysteriously labeled bottles. Then the Chief began moving briskly, talking again as he did so.

'I promised to show you how this gold business is done. Right — see here.'

He motioned to the cathode ray tube equipment and indicated the small matrix at the base of it. Into it he placed a chunk of iron, then closed the matrix door and pulled a lever that completely surrounded the matrix with lead.

'This isn't magic, you know,' he said dryly, switching on two of the generators. 'The secret of metal transmutation came in when atomic power was found. Indeed, metal transmutation is atomic power. It simply consists of forcing into a piece of matter the requisite number of electrons to make it change its material state. The cathode ray tube, linked up to that electro-magnetic equipment there, does just that.'

'You mean,' Jerry Bax said, always the brightest of the gang, 'that you've found the way to alter any material structure, so it becomes something else?'

'That's it — but in the higher orders I have much more work yet to do. Iron, for those of you who can understand me, is called iron because it is a chunk of matter having twenty-six electrons flying round the proton, or nucleus. But add fifty-three more electrons to each atomic group within the material, and you have seventy-nine altogether in each group. That piece of matter is then called gold, because of the seventy-nine electrons. In some cases, electrons are withdrawn to go from a heavier element to a lighter one. Understand me?'

The 'grandson' and Nick Gregson plainly did not, but Jerry and the elderly Larry nodded slowly. Though they were not by any means nuclear physicists, they gathered the drift and each had, at some time, heard of the Periodic table of elements.

'Yes,' the Chief mused, watching the instruments, 'we have come a long way since the days of the housebreaker, with the bull's-eye lantern and a jemmy in his hand. Crime these days is a scientific art, my friends, in every sense of the word, and nothing less than a skilled opponent can hope to beat the police, for they are not fools, either, believe me.'

'Well, you're in a position to know!' Jerry grinned.

The Chief said nothing. He calmly studied the instruments while those around him backed away slightly before the somewhat terrifying display of electrical power sizzling and flashing around them. Man-made lightning was climbing up and down magnetic pillars; the cathode ray tube was alive with lavender coruscations.

Then, at the stroke of a switch, everything ceased and the Chief opened up the matrix. From it he withdrew in a pair of tongs a chunk of gold, somewhat larger than the chunk of iron that had originally been placed there.

'If that isn't magic, I don't know what is, Chief!' the 'grandson' exclaimed, staring.

The Chief only smiled and carried the chunk across to a bench whereon stood a variety of moulds and electric furnaces.

'Here is where the job is finished,' he explained. 'The gold is correctly adulterated and . . . '

'Adulterated!' Jerry exclaimed. 'But a sovereign is pure gold, isn't it?'

'It is twenty-two parts pure gold and two parts alloy,' the Chief corrected. 'Its weight is fixed at 123.27447 grains troy. Any sovereign responding to that weight is okay — as all ours are. Loosely, one considers it pure gold, but I haven't fallen into the trap. I have made careful research. Now here, you see the various moulds, made by a master-craftsman of my acquaintance, covering various periods from 1489, when the sovereign first appeared, onwards. The heads of the various kings or queens are here in the moulds, with the appropriate die-casts of the sovereign's other side.'

Larry wrinkled his brow. 'You then melt the gold, and run it into these moulds?'

'That's it. And the cutting and milling machines you see over there. Quite a private mint, in fact. Naturally.' the Chief added, with a dry smile, 'I haven't explained the full process of transmutation. I'm not quite such a fool as that. However, you see here the basis of what promises to become a prosperous business. And we can never be caught out. We can literally make money for nothing.'

Silence. The eyes of the men were on the gold — mostly in envy. Envy that one man should know so much, and be able to give every order because of it. To kill him would be easy, but of what avail? Without his profound knowledge, nothing could be done. He was the planner of everything; he made everything, knew everything and, as yet, the law had not the remotest idea he even existed.

'Suppose,' the 'grandson' said, 'for the sake of argument, that somebody did get wise to this racket? What then?'

'That somebody would die.' The Chief gave his characteristic shrug. 'Die, my friends — painfully and completely. And none could fathom how it happened, or at least, the real cause behind it. There is nothing I have overlooked — nothing!'

2

For the time being, the work of the super counterfeiters was done. They were decided — or at least the Chief was — not to do anything further for perhaps three months. In the interval all of them returned to different walks of life to carry on a pseudo-existence as best suited the Chief. Jerry Bax was still a supposed world-traveller and lived on the fat of the land with all expenses paid, making what contacts he could find for a touch at a later date.

Larry and the 'grandson' both departed separately to France to smell out the prospect in that country, whilst Nick Gregson found himself in the dock region, doing an ordinary job of work until he should be wanted. In the case of every man there was, of course, a reason for the police wishing to find them; but they were all safe enough from actual arrest and cunning enough to keep out of harm's way.

The only one who was always in danger if he were to show his unlovely face was 'Mopes' McCall; and to him there still fell the grinding monotony of keeping a constant watch over the great mansion, fending for himself as best he could, hidden from the eyes of the law, always waiting to grab him. He was kept provided with food and drink and cigarettes by a nocturnal friend of the Chief's; but otherwise he never stirred out of the rambling old pile. His only friends were the radio and television.

Altogether, there were times when he wondered if a return to Dartmoor might not be preferable — then, recalling that he would have some fifteen years to spend there, he changed his mind. So he remained the caretaker and nursed in his subhuman brain a growing hatred for the brilliant man who was his absolute boss and jailer.

It was sheer inquisitiveness that led him to go down into the laboratory one November night. Sick to the back teeth of his own company, he was anxious for some kind of novelty — and he still smouldered at the contempt with which he had been treated by the Chief. Not the intelligence to understand, huh? Well, maybe there was an answer to that, too!

Cigarette dangling at the corner of his thick lips, his hands in his trousers pockets, he wandered down into the brightly lighted subterranean area and surveyed, smoke drifting into his left eye.

'Wonder why the mug doesn't think up a way to make a woman, same as they do on the films?' he muttered. 'That'd make this damned set-up worth while.'

He prowled around slowly, peering at this and that, feeling there were a lot of things he'd like to smash up, yet afraid to do a thing for fear of explosions and sudden death. He just couldn't find anything whereby he could hit back at the Chief and take that superior smile from his face.

'Even if I set fire to the joint, I'd only land back in the doghouse,' 'Mopes' told himself morosely. 'So maybe I shouldn't. Can't think why I can't have a maid or somethin', to help out with keepin' the place tidy.'

He knew perfectly well why, but it didn't console him much, just the same. So he just went on prowling, surveying the electric monsters and finally ending up beside the bench where lay the coin moulds for the stamping machine. Absently, he stubbed out his cigarette on the nearest mould, and then gave a gasp. He had not noticed that the mould, pipe-shaped where it fitted into the machine, with the engraving at the base, had been half over the bench edge. The sudden pressure he put on it toppled it to the floor. He stared down at it, sweat suddenly down his face. Even from here, he could see the pipe had a crack right down it and that the King Edward VII engraving had split!

'Hell!' 'Mopes' whispered, then he picked the die up and examined it. The angle at which it had fallen on the stone floor had fractured it three-quarters of the way round. When it was in use it would crumple up under the impact of striking the shiny blank sovereigns.

'Weld it,' 'Mopes' muttered, glancing urgently about him. 'That's it. Weld the crack. I'm not such a mug I can't do that.

CARDIFF
CAERDYDD

Did it back in the doghouse, in fact.'

In this he was correct. Long ago, he'd been a welder in a garage, and had pursued a similar tack in jail. Now it might even save his life, for he had little doubt that the Chief would take it out of his hide if he discovered what had happened. Down here, there was all the necessary welding equipment. Right!

'Mopes' went to work, the most careful job he had ever done. At the end of half an hour the thin crack was certainly well sealed, and well nigh undetectable, so carefully had he smoothed the rough edges of the seam away. But he had overlooked the fact that a coin mould must be absolute precision to produce the required image, therefore he looked with some misgivings upon the defaced profile of his late Majesty, King Edward VII.

'Only spot it if he looks close, and I'll not admit anything,' 'Mopes' murmured. 'Who the hell cares about a crooked nose and a bit off the beard, anyway?'

The defaced mould meant no more to him than this. He had not the wit to see what repercussions might follow. He put the mould carefully on the bench, restored the welding equipment to its rightful position, then went back upstairs before he did any more damage. An hour later he was asleep, dreaming of absolute pardon by the law, and hundreds of beautiful girls crowding round to congratulate him.

A week later the Chief returned abruptly. He merely stated he was calling a meeting; that there was a job they could pull which would need only Nick Gregson and the elderly Larry. They would be coming the next night; the Chief would be staying over to get some laboratory work done. That could only mean making coins. 'Mopes' took everything in sour silence and inwardly wondered if any King Edward VII sovereigns would be cast.

They were. The Chief worked on them all the following day, but so great was his hurry, and so sure was he of his equipment, he made no special examinations. By evening he had minted ten thousand sovereigns of King Edward VII period and suitably stained and polished them to give an impression of age. Hardly had he finished before Nick Gregson and Larry, urgently contacted, presented themselves and 'Mopes' found himself shut out of the library and detailed to prepare a supper for all three.

In consequence of this visit, an elderly 'lady' took up residence in a house in South Kensington that had long been empty. Before having her furniture brought, she sent for a gasman to check all pipes because she had a morbid fear of death through this agency. Knowing exactly what to do, Nick Gregson made a suitable hole in the floor of the empty drawing room and placed within it the aged box that contained the ten thousand gold sovereigns. This done, he went down the road to the pawnbroker's in the nearby shopping center. That Samuel Grindberg was in the market for sovereigns was obvious; the poster across his window blazoned the fact for all to see.

'I see you're interested in sovereigns, Mister,' Nick Gregson commented, as Grindberg himself came to attend to his customer.

'Right.' Grindberg surveyed Nick's uniform and was perfectly satisfied that everything was in order.

'In that case, take my tip and go and see the old lady who's moving in to seventeen, Caterham Gate. I've just bin fixin' the gas pipes, and dug up a box of sovereigns — 'undreds of 'em! King Edward Seventh, from the look of 'em. The old lady told me to ask you to go and see her. Okay?'

'Thanks — I will.'

And Samuel Grindberg wasted no time about it. He called his lady assistant to take care of the shop and then set off. Larry, superbly disguised, was smoking his pipe when the doorbell rang. Promptly he put the pipe away, assumed the shaky old woman's role, and admitted the energetic, middle-aged Grindberg into the empty ball.

'Good morning, madam. Grindberg's the name. A gas man told me about . . . '

'Some sovereigns he had found? Yes, yes, indeed . . . most remarkable.' Larry had cultivated an excellent quavering treble. 'As it was a matter of some urgency, he offered to help me out. I understand you deal in sovereigns?'

'I buy them, madam, certainly — providing they are yours to sell.'

'Well, they're on my property, so I'll take the responsibility. Come and see them for yourself.'

Grindberg nodded and followed the 'old lady' as 'she' shambled into the drawing room. In another moment he was on his knees, regardless of the dust, turning over the pile of coins in the box below floorboard level.

'No doubt of it,' he said. 'Sovereigns of Edward Seventh period.'

'Then,' Larry said, innocently, 'I would like to sell them to you.'

'Yes, and I'll be glad to buy them, providing they're genuine, and that you'll indemnify me against any police enquiry.'

'Genuine? Well, of course they're genuine!'

Grindberg picked up one of the coins and examined it carefully with a jeweller's lens. When he had finished his examination, there was a puzzled look on his face.

'I'm not altogether satisfied that these sovereigns are genuine, madam; unless, of course, their age has something to do with the defacement on the King's profile. However, we still wish to do a deal, don't we?'

'Naturally.' Larry was getting worried. This was the first time the sovereigns had ever been questioned.

'My reputation around here is impeccable,' Grindberg said, rising and dusting his knees. 'I'm prepared to give you a receipt for these sovereigns whilst I have them examined by experts. If they're perfectly genuine, I'll pay full market price for however many there may be. How's that?'

Larry reflected swiftly, only to realize almost immediately that he dared not refuse. To do so would look very suspicious. But what the devil did the man mean by questioning their genuineness? The Chief surely hadn't slipped up for once?

'Well?' Grindberg raised an eyebrow.

'Yes, that will be all right. How — how soon will you know whether you can buy them or not?'

'Oh, by this time tomorrow, I should

think. And if they are spurious, the police must be told, naturally.'

'The police?' Larry's make-up saved his look of consternation.

'Certainly — for your good, madam, and mine. You can't afford to have spurious coins on your property, any more than I can afford to be mixed up in a possible deal concerning them. Leave everything to me, Mrs. — er . . . ?'

'Mrs. Henshaw.'

'Right! Leave everything to me, Mrs. Henshaw, and I'll see we're safe enough, whatever the analysis shows.' Grindberg scribbled hastily. 'Here is your receipt, madam. I'll get back to the shop and . . . No, better still, I'll ask my son to come and remove this lot for me. He's only next door but one — a building contractor — and he has a handcart, amongst other things.'

Larry nodded rather dazedly, still painfully aware of the fact that there wasn't anything he could do. There was not even the opportunity of disappearing and taking the coins with him before things became too involved. For one thing, they were too heavy for him at his age and, for another, Grindberg had said he was only going next door but one, which was as good as him hardly being off the doorstep. But what the devil had he meant by the coins not being genuine?

Puzzled, he picked one of them up out of the box and examined it carefully. The King's head was a little out of shape, certainly, but that surely didn't mean anything? Since he was not an expert on coins, Larry was incapable of arriving at any conclusion before Grindberg returned with a powerful young man in the early twenties — obviously his son.

'I'll contact you tomorrow then, Mrs. Henshaw,' the pawnbroker smiled, as the box was dragged from the room. 'Will you be at this address?'

'I expect to be,' Larry responded. 'If I should miss you, I'll call in at your shop.'

'Fair enough. Only a few yards down the road.'

With that, Grindberg took his departure. Larry let a reasonable time elapse, then he, too, left the house, keeping up his old lady act until he reached the nearest telephone kiosk. Here he made a call.

'Chief?' he asked as, at length, there came a reply.

'What's the idea? I told you not to use this extension without vital reason.'

'There is vital reason, Chief! It's about . . .'

'Whatever it is, it can wait. Ring me in twenty minutes at my private number, then we can speak freely. That's all.'

The line clicked and became dead. Larry compressed his lips, shrugged to himself, then glanced briefly at his woman's wristwatch. For the next twenty minutes he killed time as best he could, wandering further away from the region of his 'house' all the time. The moment the twenty minutes was up, he hurried quickly to the nearest kiosk and rang the Chief's private number.

'Well, what is it?' the Chief's voice asked impatiently. 'I've had to take time out to take this call at my home, and you'd better have a good reason. Larry speaking, isn't it?'

'That's right. I thought you ought to

know that there are signs of danger. Grindberg — the likely prospect — has his suspicions about the sovereigns. He's going to have them analyzed and, if he doesn't like them, he intends to inform the police.'

'If he doesn't like them? What the hell do you mean by that? There is nothing wrong with those sovereigns.'

'He seems to think there is. Something to do with the King's face being wrong. Anyway, Chief, I don't like it. If he starts getting the police on the job, we're going to be in a fix. Or, at any rate, I am — and Nick Gregson as well. So — what's the answer?'

Silence for a while, then: 'When is Grindberg going to tell you what he thinks about the coins?'

'Tomorrow. He's taken the coins for examination and given me a receipt.' And Larry added all the details.

'I cannot imagine why he should have a reason for suspicion,' the Chief observed at length, thoughtfully. 'If there is a reason, and he goes to the police, we'll certainly be in an awkward position. They have unpleasantly efficient methods of finding things out. Let me think, now — Grindberg will undoubtedly phone the police if he has a reason, therefore he will not leave his premises and make himself available for us to get at him.'

'Get at him?' Larry repeated.

'That's what I said. There is suspicion in that man's mind, Larry, and he'll magnify every little defect in the coins for that reason. He's got to be stopped, and we've got to have those sovereigns back for examination. You can leave this to me. Best thing you can do is to drop out of sight, resume your normal identity and go to the hideout in Ireland. I'll let you know when I want you. I've got to move fast.'

'Right,' Larry responded promptly, thankful to be able to drop out of the proceedings, and he rang off.

At the other end of the line the Chief sat musing for a moment or two, then he picked up the phone again. It was the thick argumentative voice of 'Mopes' that answered him — very cautiously to commence with.

'A job for you, 'Mopes',' the Chief said

briefly. 'Get the closed saloon from the house garage and use your usual moustache and glasses disguise. You'll be safe enough at the wheel of the car. You'll drive it to Caterham Gate, South Kensington, and stop at the corner of Alderson Street. There you will pick up Nick Gregson. I'll make arrangements for him to be there. Got that so far?'

'Yep,' 'Mopes' agreed heavily. 'Be a relief to get out of this damned joint.'

'I haven't finished yet. Listen further. This is an elimination job . . . '

'The snake stuff!' 'Mopes' cried eagerly.

'That's it. You'll find everything in the laboratory, second shelf up. Take it with you. The man you will eliminate is named Grindberg. He runs a jewellery and pawnbrokers shop just beyond the Alderson Street corner. I'll arrange that he leaves that shop around noon. He's middle-aged, active in his walk, becoming bald, with a fresh complexion. Make sure it *is* him before you do anything. Let Nick do the driving. Transfer Grindberg's body to anywhere you like, so long as it's off the beaten track. Has that much registered?'

'Yep.'

'Lastly, you will return to Grindberg's shop. I don't think there'll be anybody there, except a young woman. Silence her somehow, so she can't identify you later, but you are not, under any circumstances, to harm her. In that shop, somewhere, you'll find there are ten thousand sovereigns. Get them — and get back to the house by night — not day. That will be around seven at this time of year. Everything clear?'

'Yep.'

The Chief pressed down the receiver rest, waited, then let it rise again. From the directory he rang Grindberg's number.

'Hello, yes? Grindberg, jeweller, speaking.'

'Would you be interested in viewing a selection of diamond rings, Mr. Grindberg?' the Chief asked in a polite voice.

'Are they valuable?'

'As a collector, I would place their total worth at about two hundred thousand pounds. I have a few other gem dealers who will be coming to my home later. I've included you on the list.'

'Kind of you,' Grindberg said, 'but why? Do I know you? Do you know me?'

'I know you quite well, and have been impressed by your fair prices for precious stones. Of course, if you're not interested . . .'

'Hold on a minute. Who says I'm not interested? A gem dealer is always interested in diamonds. What is your name, sir?'

'Andrew Carmichael.'

Grindberg gave a little gasp and then blinked. Andrew Carmichael was one of the greatest buyers of gems in the city. Then the ever-suspicious Grindberg remembered something.

'I read the other day that Andrew Carmichael had gone to the continent.'

'Publicity stuff,' the Chief responded calmly. 'I prefer to drop out of sight now and again whilst I finish special deals. Let me tell you, Mr. Grindberg, that this is a very special offer. Do you wish to view these diamonds, along with your competitors, or don't you?'

'Of course I do. When would be convenient?'

'Be at my home at two o'clock this afternoon. Elm Terrace, West One. The Larches.'

'Two o'clock is a bit difficult . . . '

'That is the only time when you can see the stuff without your competitors also being present. I have all the times arranged. If, of course, you buy on the spot, I'll cancel the others.'

Grindberg was a businessman. 'I'll be there!'

He rang off and glanced at his watch. He had only time to get lunch and then be on his way. His intention to make a thorough examination of 'Mrs. Henshaw's' sovereigns would have to wait until later. Turning, he raised his voice in a shout:

'Betty!'

A slim, good-looking girl in the early twenties — exactly the right type to tell the tale to the customers — came hurrying into his back office.

'Yes, Mr. Grindberg?'

'Better close for lunch. You'll have to take over for most of this afternoon. I've some important business in the city.'

'Yes, Mr. Grindberg,' and the attractive blonde took her departure and returned on time to open the shop up again. As he had intimated, Grindberg was missing.

Until three o'clock, nothing happened in Mr. Grindberg's establishment. The implicitly trusted Betty manicured her faultless nails, ate six chocolate nougats, read part of her romantic novel and imagined herself swept into the arms of a laughing Caribbean brigand — then came two customers. Muttering to herself, she switched on her dazzling smile and drifted to a position behind the nearest glass showcase.

'Good afternoon, gentlemen,' she greeted brightly, but as there was no response, something of the smile faded from her face. The two men had come in and turned their backs to her to examine another showcase. Now they turned to face her, she realized they were masked with handkerchiefs. One of them was small and the other huge. Both wore overcoats with upturned collars and soft hats low down over their eyes. To recognize any features was impossible.

Betty was plainly and simply scared to death, but she still had the presence of mind to remember the button to the burglar alarm. Her delicate white hand began to stray to it, until the massive paw of 'Mopes' crashed down on her wrist.

'Better not,' he muttered, as the girl flushed with pain. 'Get back out of sight — behind them cabinets.'

'Look here — who do you think you're ordering about — eh?'

Betty wondered how she had the nerve to say that much. The next moment she was seized and bundled behind the cabinets. 'Mopes' powerful hands held her tightly against the wall.

'Hurry it up, Nick,' 'Mopes' snapped, forgetting he ought not to use names. 'Find them sovs. and let's get out.'

'Why not yell it out in the street that we're here, an' be done with it?' Nick blazed. 'You've shouted my name, and what we've come for. Anything else?'

'Search — and shut up! Sugar here won't say nothin', will you?' And 'Mopes' shook the girl fiercely.

'No — no, of course I won't!' Her blue

eyes were wide in fright as 'Mopes' still pinned her against the wall. She did her best to try and discern his features, but it was impossible. All she could clearly detect were his cold, blue, inexorable eyes. They were studying her intently, almost inhumanly.

Then he suddenly looked away and watched Nick's urgent searching in the back office.

'There's sovereigns in this joint some place,' Mopes said abruptly. 'You look the bright sort uv girl who'd know just where. How's about telling me, huh?'

'I don't know . . . ' Betty gasped, her eyes watering as 'Mopes' smashed a hand viciously across her face.

'Don't hand me that, sugar. You're a trusty in this joint, or you wouldn't be left with all this caboodle. Where is it? The sovereigns, I mean! Cough it up before I bash your pretty top through that showcase!'

At that, Betty found herself swung around helplessly, lifted off her feet, so the showcase was perilously near her face.

'The — the safe!' she gasped hoarsely.

'They're in the safe. In — in a box.'

'Mopes' set her down. 'What's the combination?'

'I — I . . .'

'Quick, damn you — ! We haven't no time to waste!'

'Left four, right six, left two — and let go of me!' she panted, struggling. 'Get your filthy hands off me!'

'Not just yet, sugar. Got that combination, Nick? Hurry it up!' 'Mopes' turned back to the girl and whirled her back again against the wall. 'Y' know something, sugar? You're just the kind of kid I could go for. I'll show you what I mean. I hold you tighter up against me, like this, see, and with my right hand I — hell!' 'Mopes' broke off as, in shifting his hand, the girl's right arm was also released and she made good use of it.

Her right hand gouged down his face, tearing away the handkerchief mask and ripping the flesh down his cheek. For the moment 'Mopes' forgot his lustful intentions and realized two other things instead. His features were revealed, and he was bleeding like hell. Then the girl had twisted and torn free of his remaining hand.

She blundered towards the shop doorway, screaming at the top of her voice. She grabbed the door to open it — but 'Mopes' was upon her.

'You hell-fired she-cat!' he yelled. 'Stick your claws in me, will you?'

His terrific right fist slammed straight into her jaw as she swung round, and that did it. 'Mopes' was an immensely powerful man, with all the brute force that often goes with a turgid intelligence. Betty was literally lifted from her feet under the impact of the blow, her brain crashing into darkness. She hit the showcase behind her, recoiled from its wooden edge without breaking the glass, then crashed on her face on the floor and lay motionless. The whole thing took only a few seconds, and 'Mopes' watched it all in fascination. Then he glanced at the closed door.

Two people were looking at the articles in the window. But were barred from seeing into the shop by the array of goods.

They might come in at any moment, thought 'Mopes' moved, with some intelligence for once. He took one leap at the door, jammed the bolt, then retreated without being noticed.

Striding over the girl's motionless body, he looked in at the office doorway.

'Hurry it up, Nick! How in hell much longer?'

Nick turned from levering a heavy box out of the safe. Then he gave a start.

'Your mask! Where is it?'

'The bitch scratched it off. Got that stuff yet?'

'Yes, but it'll take both of us . . . What wus that you said about the kid?'

'I had to quieten her. She got tough . . .'

A startled look came into Nick's eyes. Suddenly abandoning his effort with the case of sovereigns, he brushed past the ponderous 'Mopes' and hurried into the shop. In a matter of seconds he spotted the girl and dropped beside her.

'You damned silly fool!' he whispered, getting up again slowly. 'This kid's dead. Dead! You know what the Chief said 'bout not hurting her.'

'Dead?' A vague look of alarm came to Mopes' unlovely face. 'She can't be! I only tapped her on the chin for ploughin' my face up.'

'Her neck's broken, anyway.' Sweating, Nick gave a quick glance about him, towards the people passing up and down in the street outside. Then he swung back to 'Mopes'.

'We've only one chance, since you've ballsed up the whole thing, 'Mopes'. Make it look like a robbery. Take some of the stuff in here as well as the sovereigns. Shove the kid behind the counter outa sight.'

'Mopes' moved like a Juggernaut. He dragged the dead girl behind the counter and then stuffed his pockets with small valuables, while Nick did likewise.

'Right!' Nick panted. 'That's all we can do. Get the door open. We'll walk out, carry the case between us. No masks, though, any more than when we came in. That'd get folks wonderin'. As it is, we oughta make it.'

'Mopes' ripped off his kerchief from

57

around his neck and jammed it in his pocket, then he headed into the office. Nick followed him, to find he was not needed. With a red face and a good deal of hard breathing, 'Mopes' hauled the case on to his shoulder.

'Take two uv us!' he sneered. 'Why in hell don't you get some muscle in that rat's body of yours? Get the door open.'

Nick nodded briefly and hurried forward to pull back the bolt. The door swung open. As casually as possible, keeping their faces averted, they left the shop and moved to their car at the kerb, a few yards away.

'Mopes' heaved the case of sovereigns into the front seat with such force it ripped the hide. Five seconds later he and Nick were on their way, and men and women still passed back and forth outside Grindberg's shop, unaware that anything unusual had happened.

3

The sensation-mongers had plenty to feast on in the evening papers. The choice of two intriguing items. The *Record* chose 'KENSINGTON MURDER ROBBERY' for its headline, whilst the *Echo* preferred 'PAWNBROKER DIES OF SNAKEBITE'.

The *Echo*, in fact, considered it so unusual for a man in a disused warehouse to be found dead from snakebite that they ran a feature about it. Death from a snake had not happened in England since — oh, heaven knew when! Reporters went grey trying to find the last occasion. But what connection had a pawnbroker dead from snakebite to do with his own shop being robbed and his girl assistant being killed? Was it coincidence or deliberate plotting? Had the gold sovereign found on the dead pawnbroker anything to do with the mystery? This was what the police wanted to know.

In fact, it was what everybody wanted to know.

And, in a certain mansion, thirty miles from London, the Chief was on the rampage. Cloistered with 'Mopes' McCall and Nick Gregson in the library, he had about exhausted all the epithets he could think of in expressing his fury.

'I should think you've done every damned thing I told you not to do!' was his final explosion.

'Just the way things 'appened, Chief,' Nick muttered sullenly.

'I'm not blaming you, Nick, so much as this thick-eared clod who worked with you. Blast you, 'Mopes', what did you have to kill that girl for?'

'Mopes' moved uneasily. 'I didn't do it on purpose, Chief. I only tapped her on the chin . . . '

'Why?'

'She wus goin' to give things away by shoutin' inter the street. It wus the only thing I could do.'

'She broke her neck, anyway,' the Chief snapped. 'And I expect you left your damned fingerprints all over the place

— and on her, or I don't know you! You are already fingerprinted as a convicted criminal. I can see there may be a row over this lot, 'Mopes', and if there is, I'll see that you're in it up to your neck. It was to avoid anything like this that I gave orders for the girl assistant not to be hurt. That's murder, you dim-witted ape — or didn't you know?'

'So wus bumpin' off Grindberg!' 'Mopes' retorted.

'I agree — but nobody will be able to trace that, providing you did the job properly.'

'We did everything you said, Chief,' Nick said nervously. 'Picked him up when he left the shop and took him to an empty warehouse. Then we 'snake-bited' him, just like you said.'

The Chief looked at the box of sovereigns on the floor of the library. Picking one of them up, he examined it under the bright desk light. Quickly he turned back again and picked up a handful. By the time he had finished studying each coin in turn, his face was grim.

'This is wonderful!' he declared sourly, flinging them back in the box. 'If the sovereign found on Grindberg was identical with these, the prospect of trouble is about trebled. For some reason, each one of these sovereigns is wrongly cast.'

'Can't blame us for that, Chief,' 'Mopes' commented.

The Chief did not answer. He thought for a moment or two; then, suddenly making up his mind, he hurried from the library, slamming the door behind him. He went straight down into the laboratory and across to the bench where lay the moulds. In a few minutes he was back, bringing with him the faulty mould for King Edward VII.

'What's the answer to this, 'Mopes'?' he asked curtly.

'Mopes' looked at the mould, then at the Chiefs steely eyes. He rubbed the end of his bulbous nose rather uncertainly.

'I — I dunno, boss. What is it?'

'A mould, welded up the centre,' the Chief sneered. 'I didn't do it, and you're the only person around here in the normal way. This welded crack has spoiled the profile impression, and the flaw has repeated in every sovereign that has been cast. I never noticed it at the time, because I was too busy. Thanks to Grindberg having one of the sovereigns on his person, the police are going to think things.'

'Mopes' breathed hard. 'I — I didn't know I'd done anything wrong, Chief. I heard a noise below and went to look. Me hand caught the mould and knocked it on to the floor. So — so I repaired it.'

'Without telling me!'

'I — I wus scared uv what you'd say, or do.'

'There's nothing I can do — it's done.' The Chief put the mould on the table and sighed. 'No use my taking it out of your hide, 'Mopes', you're too thick-skinned. But one day I may pay you back when you don't expect it. For the moment, the unpleasant truth is that our whole organization has been thrown into chaos, and the police are probably sniffing out our trail at this very moment. I'll do what I can to deflect them, but it won't be easy.

You'll stay on here, 'Mopes', and keep guard. You, Nick, had better be on your way whilst it's dark. Go back to your usual job and I'll tell you when you're needed. If there's trouble about your being away from your job, let me know. I'll square it for you.'

Nick gave a quick nod and beat a retreat, glad to get away from the Chief's smouldering rage. 'Mopes' remained unmoved, far too obtuse to realize that, one day, the Chief would strike him down without mercy.

It was also about this time that Chief-Inspector Norden, of the Yard's murder squad, was pondering the sovereign lying on his blotter. Save for the faint clicking of Detective-Sergeant Withers' keyboard in the far corner as he tabulated the details of the Grindberg shop murder, there was not a sound in the office. The dusty electric light was glowing and, outside, was the gloom of the late autumn night hovering over the Embankment across the way.

'The point is,' Norden said at last, 'is there a connection between the death of

Grindberg himself from snakebite, and the murder of his girl assistant? Viewed impartially, the two things don't seem to be connected. Yet, looking at this sovereign, I begin to wonder.'

'Yes, sir,' Withers said dutifully, and went on with his typing. He was accustomed to his superior's habit of thinking out loud.

After a while, Norden drew to him the police surgeon's report and read it through for the third time:

'Post Mortem Report on Betty Lathom, Dec'd.

Cause of death I ascribe to fracture of the vertebrae, possibly caused in the first instance by a severe blow to the jaw, which caused the head to jerk back sharply. The blow was probably administered by a fist, since there are no marks to suggest an instrument. It is also possible that the deceased was hit in the face, there being distinct evidence of contusion on the left cheek (suggesting a right-handed attacker).'

'Mmmmm,' Norden commented to himself, and unearthed a second report.

'Post Mortem Report on Samuel Grindberg Dec'd. Cause of death I ascribe to severe snakebite, though from what kind of snake cannot be stated until further analysis of the venom within the victim has been made. No other traces of injury.'

'Fatal snakebite in Britain. It's unheard of.' Norden was talking aloud again. 'If I could only be sure that the snake-bite business is phony, cleverly arranged murder, I could also be sure that the raid on the Grindberg shop was part of the same set-up.'

He reached to the interphone and switched through to the Fingerprint Records department

'Dabs? That you, Harry? Anything checking yet on those prints you got at Grindberg's?'

'I'm just coming round, sir. I think we've something that will interest you.'

'Good! About time somebody had!'

In a moment or two the fingerprint expert had arrived, carrying with him an indexed folder. Laying it on the desk, he opened it at a photograph — a complete record indeed, including fingerprints — of one 'Mopes' McCall.

'No doubt of one thing, sir,' the expert said. 'The few prints we found in Grindberg's are all identical with those of this chap. Other prints are obviously made by gloves. Seems unlikely McCall here would wear gloves part of the time only. Which suggests he had an accomplice, or accomplices.'

'Uh-huh.' Norden studied the photograph. 'Ugly looking cuss, isn't he? Escaped Dartmoor two years ago, did he? Not recaptured. Mmmm. No record of him being mixed up in counterfeit coins, I suppose?'

'No, sir. Before he was convicted for robbery and attempted murder — and those other charges you see on his record there — he was a panel-beater and welder in an obscure garage somewhere.'

'Right. That's all I need at the moment, Harry. But thanks very much — and leave the file here.'

The expert nodded and went out. In the corner, at his own desk, Withers went on typing steadily, wondering just how soon it would be possible to knock off work. It was already ten past eight.

'It seems to me,' Norden said presently, as though he had read the sergeant's thoughts, 'that there's not much more we can do tonight, Jim. I want the full report on Grindberg, for one thing, and a statement from the Royal Mint concerning this sovereign for another. Nothing much more we can do for the moment.'

With which Withers promptly agreed and, ten minutes later, both he and Norden had returned to their homes, to forget all about murder, snake-bites and robbery; but, the following morning, they were back on the job again — or, at least, Withers was. His superior did not arrive until nearly eleven o'clock, and then it was with a puzzled look on his square face.

'Morning. Jim,' he greeted briefly. 'Anything more yet?' he added, pulling off his overcoat.

'No, sir. I've got the reports complete on the Grindberg business, and Doc. Andrews has sent in a further report on Grindberg. Seems it was rattlesnake venom that killed him.'

'Rattlesnake? Wonder how the hell an American serpent got over here ... ' Norden crossed to the desk and studied the report thoughtfully.

'Rider on Post Mortem of Samuel Grindberg Dec'd. It is my opinion, after chemical analysis of the deceased's bloodstream, that death was caused by rattlesnake venom, within approximately ninety minutes of the bite.

'Closer investigation of the corpse reveals two small punctures at the base of the throat, which tally with the width of a rattlesnake's poison fangs.'

'Think of that!' Norden commented and, sitting down, he lifted the telephone. 'Get me the chief caretaker at the Zoological Gardens, please, and make it quick.'

Returning the phone to its rest, he took from his pocket the solitary golden sovereign he had been inspecting the previous evening. Detective-Sergeant Withers raised a questioning eyebrow.

'The Royal Mint never manufactured this coin, Jim,' Norden said, holding it up.

'I checked on it this morning, which is where I've been till now. On the other hand the metallurgy department tells me it contains all the necessary ingredients of a sovereign.'

'Right amount of gold, you mean?'

'Right amount of gold and alloy.'

'Well, then — doesn't that make it legal tender?'

Norden looked severe. 'My dear man, where have you lived? Any coin which has not been produced by the Royal Mint is spurious. Dammit, if we had people turning out gold sovereigns just as they liked — correct proportion of gold and alloy notwithstanding — where would we be? This is a fake. Why Grindberg had it in his pocket, and whether it is connected with the murder of that poor girl Betty Lathom we don't know — but we may soon. I have Grindberg's son, Nathaniel, coming in this morning. He was out of town yesterday, so we couldn't get a statement from him . . .'

Norden broke off and lifted the telephone. 'Yes? Oh, yes — put him on. Zoo Supervisor? This is Chief Inspector

Norden, C.I.D., Metropolitan Division. I'm busy on the Grindberg case. Maybe you read the facts? Uh-huh. Yes, well, that helps a lot. Grindberg was killed by a rattlesnake, apparently. Is there one missing from the zoo — or any of the zoos — that you know of? There isn't? No information about it? Yes, I see. Tell me, how long does a rattlesnake's bite take to prove fatal? Right. Yes — I see how you mean. Many thanks.'

Norden rang off.

'No escapes from the zoos, sir?' Withers asked.

'Nothing at all and, if there had been, it would have been reported, naturally. Further, I'm not sure but that the captive snakes have their fangs drawn, anyway. But I was given the possible solution that the snake may have come over from America in some cargo somehow and escaped unnoticed — but that it happened to pick on Grindberg is the most amazing thing ever. Time of death from the bite varies from an hour to three hours, and as a rule it is fatal.'

'Whale of a queer business this, sir.'

Norden was about to answer when the door opened. 'A Mr. Nathaniel Grindberg to see you, Inspector.'

'Ah, yes. Show him in, please.' Norden got to his feet and held out his hand in welcome as the powerfully built son of the dead pawnbroker came in swiftly.

'My condolences, Mr. Grindberg,' Norden said, with a sympathetic smile. 'Have a seat . . .'

Nathaniel sat, fidgeting nervously. Norden summed him up briefly as he gradually calmed, then:

'Primarily, of course, we are investigating the murder and robbery in your late father's shop, Mr. Grindberg, but we are also trying to tie up the problem of your father's peculiar demise by snakebite. It was reported to the police in the first place by boys playing in an old warehouse, who found the body. Up to now, there has been no suspicion of foul play; just, shall we say, death from misadventure. But the way things are shaping, the inquests on both your father and Miss Lathom will be adjourned, pending further enquiry. There may be a connection.'

'Possibly.' the young man muttered. 'But I can't think what. I know I'd like to get my hands on the swine who killed Betty. We were going to become engaged next year.'

'I see . . . ' Norden picked up the sovereign from the desk. 'Have you any idea where this came from? As you will know, it was found in your father's pocket.'

'I know.' Nathaniel gave a gloomy nod. 'It'd be one of the ten thousand he took from Mrs. Henshaw for examination before buying them.'

Withers looked up sharply from making notes of the conversation. On Norden's face there was no change of expression.

'Ten thousand of them? That's a tremendous number of sovereigns. How do you know about them?'

Nathaniel gave the facts. Then: 'I'm surprised you don't know about them. They'll be in my father's safe in his office, I expect. I wanted to check on it myself, but the policeman on duty wouldn't allow me.'

'Only doing his duty, Mr. Grindberg.

This Mrs. Henshaw, from whom you took the sovereigns on your handcart; what did she look like?'

'Oh, around eighty, I'd say. Very bent, high-pitched voice, old-fashioned clothes. Seems the gas man found the sovereigns in the first place and he went and told dad, at Mrs. Henshaw's request, of course.'

'Why your father, specifically?'

'No idea. Because he was the nearest pawnbroker, I suppose.'

'I see.' Norden knocked the ashes from his pipe. 'And this elderly lady had bought number seventeen Caterham Gate, had she? And your father was to report on the sovereigns to her today?'

'That's it. Maybe she doesn't know what's happened, and is still waiting for him.'

'She will very soon be acquainted with the facts,' Norden said. 'Man from the gas company to check the pipes, lay on the gas, or what?'

'No idea of the reason for his visit, Inspector.'

Norden smiled. 'Well, thank you, Mr.

Grindberg. I shan't need to detain you any further. I'll keep in touch with you. You've no particular information you can give about Betty Lathom, I expect?'

'Afraid not. You'll have got practically everything from her parents, haven't you?'

'Yes; we did that yesterday. Her address was on her insurance card. Well, good day, Mr. Grindberg.'

Nathaniel shook hands and departed, leaving Norden looking thoughtful. He wandered back to the desk and met Withers' excited glance.

'Ten thousand sovereigns, sir! And all duds, if they are like that spare one we found on Grindberg. But they were not in the safe, even though young Nat evidently thought they were. Unless he's up to something.'

'I don't think so, Jim — though, in our job, we can't trust anybody by appearances. The point is,' Norden continued, wagging a finger, 'this business begins to make sense. We have our tie-up. Those sovereigns were taken from Grindberg's safe, obviously, and that means that the other odd articles were probably only taken for effect. But for Grindberg's son, we'd never have known there were any more sovereigns. It definitely begins to look as though the sovereigns and Grindberg's death from snakebite were all part of the same thing. The girl was perhaps wiped out to stop her talking.'

'And this Mrs. Henshaw? She's a new one.'

'Yes. Hop over to seventeen Caterham Gate, Jim, and see what you can dig up. I'll check on the gas authority and see if we can trace that gas man.'

'Right, sir.'

Withers whipped up his coat and hurried out as Norden crossed to the phone.

Before long he was in touch with the right quarter in the gas company, and he was not particularly surprised, either, when he learned that no official from the gas company had ever been sent to seventeen Caterham Gate.

Norden sat musing for a while when he had this response; then he looked through the reports, the photographs, the fingerprint records: Finally he picked up the sovereign.

'Doesn't make sense,' he muttered. 'No man would make ten thousand sovereigns of the right gold and alloy amounts, and then go through all this palaver . . . ' He switched on the interphone. 'That you, Mort? Can you spare a moment for a vital conversation?'

'No — but I'll come, just the same. I know you would hardly be asking for me unless you were out of your depth — and I love seeing you murder boys eating humble pie.'

Norden switched off, smiling sourly to himself. After a while, Chief-Inspector Mortimer Dawson presented himself. He was tall, thin and keen-featured and, from his generally jovial manner it would have been difficult to realize that he was one of the Yard's 'boffins'. In other words, he was one of three Inspectors specially versed in scientific problems and, as such, was attached to the C.I.D.'s Scientific Division.

'All right, I'm listening.' he said, throwing himself in the nearest chair and settling comfortably. 'What's on your mind, Arthur?'

'The Grindberg business, to be exact. You said I was getting out of my depth, and you're dead right! The possibility is that the prime mover in the business is minting sovereigns — ten thousand of them that I know of. And the rub is that they're exactly right in weight, gold content, and all the rest of it. What kind of a lunatic would risk that? What would he get out of it'? Cost him more to fake the damned things than to sell them.'

'Depending.' Dawson replied, 'on how he did it. His method of manufacture, I mean. You're sure all ten thousand are what you might call 'genuine duds'?'

'Here's one of the ten thousand. I can't guarantee all the others are like this, but it's an even chance that they are.'

Dawson took the coin handed to him and studied it with the eye of a specialist. Then he tossed it up and down in his palm.

'I take your word for it that the contents are right?'

'Not my word, Mort — the Mint's. I had it checked there. Now, what can I do? How can a man manufacture this sort of thing?'

'Poor nose and beard on the profile,' Dawson mused, still scrutinizing the coin. 'Eh? How could they be manufactured? Very easily, if the secret happens to be known. I could do it myself if I knew the secret, and retire from this hell-fired business of working out other Inspectors' sums for them.'

'Would you mind coming to the point?' Norden demanded with sulphuric calm.

'All right. The answer's transmutation — I think.'

Norden wrinkled his brow. 'Isn't that something to do with souls?'

'That, my learned friend, is transmigration — a very different matter. Transmutation is the atomic theory, the Philosopher's Stone of old-fashioned alchemy — the power to change other metals into gold.'

'It's damned impossible!'

'Nothing is that, if you have a scientific mind. The scientists have striven for years to discover a way of changing one metal into another, even more so since the atomic theory came in. It is a controlled principle of adding or subtracting electrons from atoms of matter, thereby altering their constitution. A man who could do that — a brilliant nuclear physicist, for instance — could make a sovereign like this. Thousands or tens of thousands, like stamping out confetti from paper.'

'But — but you don't seriously mean that some criminal scientist is doing that?'

'In this space and atomic age I can't think why not. The cost to him would be heavy — yes; but negligible, compared to the profit he'd make with those things in circulation. From what I can see, he's slipped up in the die-cast somewhere, and that's exposed the whole thing.'

Norden sighed and then irritably refilled his pipe. 'Now I'm getting really sunk! I'm a straightforward murder man, with my murder box, lens, and band of helpers. I've never had a case I couldn't solve, but if I'm getting entangled with nuclear physicists who can turn things into gold — I'm quitting!'

Dawson grinned and tossed the coin back on the table. 'You can't quit. The Assistant Commissioner takes a dim view of that kind of thing.'

'I can transfer the case to a specialist. Yourself, for instance . . . Yes,' Norden went on, musing, 'you know, Mort, the more I think of it, the more scientific this business becomes. The death of Grindberg, for instance, from the bite of a rattlesnake. Everything pathological says a rattlesnake did it, but somehow, I can't believe it. Whoever heard of a rattlesnake in the heart of London? Nobody else has been bitten, or else it hasn't been reported, and no snakes are missing from the zoo. Do you think a snakebite could be faked in some way?'

'Surely.' Dawson apparently had no doubt about it. He spread his hands. 'You only want the venom and something that looks like snakebite — and there you are; at least, I think so. I'm a scientist, not a specialized pathologist. Let's have Ensdale's view. He's the smartest pathologist and physicist we've got on the staff.'

Norden turned to the intercom and gave the necessary instructions; then they had to bide their time until Boyd Ensdale saw fit to grace the drab office with his presence. He was head of the pathology division and acting consultant to the scientists, quite one of the cleverest men at the Yard. His degrees ran into two columns of small type in 'Who's Who'.

His appearance, when he arrived, bore no relation to his position or knowledge. He was of small build, untidy and with graying hair that looked as though nothing on earth would keep it under control. His features were nondescript but there was intelligence in the rapier-sharp gray eyes.

'Yes, gentlemen?' he asked briefly, wandering in and perching absent-mindedly on the edge of the desk. 'Is there something you want?'

'Quite a deal, Mr. Ensdale, if you can spare the time for it.' There was unction in Norden's voice. 'It's the Grindberg case. It's taken a turn into the scientific regions.'

'Grindberg? Oh, yes — the snakebite business.'

'Exactly — the snakebite business,' Norden agreed. 'I can't credit that the snake-biting is genuine, and I'd like your opinion on whether such a thing could be faked.'

'Simple enough, I should think. You only need two needle-like prongs duplicating the width of the snake's double tongue, coat the prongs in venom, and there you are.'

'If you were to examine the body of Grindberg could you tell from the fatal wound he received whether it is genuine or a fake?'

'It might be possible by micro-analysis of the wound tissue. If it is genuine, some traces of saliva from the snake will probably be obvious. If it is not genuine, no such sign will be present. Do you wish me to look?'

'I'd be glad if you would,' Norden assented. 'Andrews is working on the corpse at the moment in the mortuary. I'll have a word with him and tell him you'll be coming over.'

'Right,' Ensdale said, slipping off the table. 'I'll let you know all about it as soon as I can.'

He left the office in the same thoughtful way as he had entered it. The door had hardly closed behind him before the telephone rang. It was Detective-Sergeant Withers at the other end of the wire.

'Nothing doing at seventeen Caterham Gate, sir,' he announced. 'Place is empty and locked up. According to neighbors, nobody has been seen near the place so far today.'

'Not very surprising,' Norden replied. 'Since the man from the gas company was also a fake, I assume Mrs. Henshaw was, as well. You'd better trace the agents who sold the house to Mrs. Henshaw and see if you . . . '

'I already have, sir. A 'For Sale' notice had been stripped down from a top window and was lying on the floor. They're in the same road — Caterham Gate — and they . . . '

'To the point, Jim. What did they say?'

'Apparently, Mrs. Henshaw hadn't bought the place. She had only been given the key and a permit to view, said permit having a time expiry of two days. Evidently just long enough for her to complete her business with Grindberg.

Needless to say, the key has not been returned to the agents' office.'

'Anything else?'

'Yes. From what I have been able to find out, Grindberg senior wasn't exactly the soul of honour.'

'So I imagine — otherwise, he wouldn't have agreed to a deal in sovereigns about the origin of which he was by no means sure. All right, Jim, thanks. You might as well come back to the office.'

Norden switched off and glanced across at Dawson.

'Plainly,' Dawson said, 'the whole thing is quite nicely organized from beginning to end. Still feel that you'd prefer me to take the job over?'

'Definitely! Give me a straightforward killing, not a modern Midas. I want you to come with me to the A.C., and I'll try and get him to let me transfer the case to you.'

The Assistant Commissioner raised no objections, and Norden's relief was obvious as he handed over all records, notes and photographs to date. It had got to evening before Dawson, by now acquainted with the main facts, received the awaited report of Boyd Ensdale. It said:

'Concerning Samuel Grindberg Dec'd — it is my opinion that the snakebite wound is genuine. Micro-analysis of tissue from around the wound reveals traces of snake saliva, along with the venom.'

Dawson put the report on one side. Detective-Sergeant Harriday, his right-hand man and also specially trained in the scientific group, picked up the report and studied it for himself.

'Genuine, after all, sir. Damned amazing coincidence — don't you think?'

'Too amazing. I don't believe it. I'm not doubting Ensdale's word, but I do think we're up against a criminal scientist with an uncanny gift for faking his effects to cover his traces. Tomorrow, in the daylight, we're going round to examine the warehouse where Grindberg was found.'

4

To the surprise of 'Mopes', the Chief paid an unexpected visit to the mansion two days after the snakebite death of Samuel Grindberg. As usual, he came by night and walked in on the strong-arm man to find him listening to the radio, his feet propped on the arm of one of the best chairs.

'Shut that thing off!' the Chief ordered.

'Sure thing.' 'Mopes' obeyed and then looked surprised. 'I thought you didn't mind me 'aving the radio and telly, boss?'

'I don't — but not that loud. How would you expect to hear anybody prowling about? You didn't even hear me.'

'I never thought of that,' 'Mopes' admitted, scratching his head.

The Chief settled himself in the nearest chair. Discreetly, 'Mopes' put his feet on the floor.

'Something wrong, Chief?' he asked presently. 'I didn't expect you comin'.'

'So I noticed, with your number twelves defiling the furniture. As for there being something wrong — yes, there is. All traceable to you. First, the damaged mould which gave away the sovereign racket; then the killing of that youngster, Betty Lathom. I've a mind to rub you out, 'Mopes'.'

The other man's eyes hardened. He was prepared to fight for his life if he had to, but he much preferred the easier way of just taking orders.

'Right now, you can be useful,' the Chief continued, musing. 'I don't know whether you've heard about it on that radio or not, but the Grindberg business has been transferred to Chief-Inspector Dawson, of the Yard's scientific division. And I don't like it. He's dangerous. Got more knowledge in his little finger than an ordinary copper has in his whole brain-box. We've got to make ourselves reasonably safe, 'Mopes'.'

'Anything you say, Chief.'

'Dawson has put it out to the press that, although all pathological reports show that Grindberg died of the venom of a rattlesnake, he doesn't believe it, and he's going to leave nothing unturned to prove that the 'bite' was deliberately created by artificial means. That can get you — and, in time, all of us — in a sticky mess, my friend.'

'Uh-huh. What do I do, then? Watch out for this mug Dawson and rub him out?'

The Chief tightened his lips impatiently.

'No! And stop being so damned crude. You'd only make things worse by killing a Yard man — and a special scientific fellow, at that. I've thought it out, and I think we can save ourselves by having three more killings at widely separated places. Not too widely, though. By that, I mean not all of them in one spot.'

'Mopes' sat listening, the set of his thick lips showing he had not in the least gathered the drift as yet.

'Dawson thinks the snakebite was phony, apparently because Grindberg happened to be the victim. He might incline to thinking it was coincidence if three other people, quite unconnected with Grindberg, also die of snakebite. The death of all all four would then be lumped together as being caused by a solitary rattlesnake loose somewhere in the city. It would probably swing things away from us.'

'Could be,' 'Mopes' admitted, after a spell of profound concentration. 'Make it look natural-like.'

'Exactly. And that's where you come into it. I want you to select three people at random, all within a quarter mile area of each other, and 'snake-bite' 'em. Tonight, for preference. You shouldn't have any difficulty.'

'Okay,' 'Mopes' growled. 'Anything else?'

'No. Get on with the job and return here . . . ' The Chief got to his feet. 'I'll be round again in due course, when I have need. At the moment we've all got to lie low until the heat's off. For some things, I wish I hadn't to trust so much to you, but it can't be helped. Oh, fresh provisions will be sent in for you tomorrow by the usual firm.'

With a nod the Chief went on his way

and a moment or two afterwards, the front door of the mansion was slammed. 'Mopes' lighted a cigarette and hummed a tune to himself as he hurried down into the laboratory. He was pleased at the prospect of a night out.

From the shelf of the bottles he took down the simple instrument for making the 'snakebite', examining it carefully. It consisted of a stainless steel blowpipe, with a double end, exactly spaced so it was the width of a snake's twin-tongued fangs. Or rather, it was slightly under the required width since it was, in basis, a blowpipe, and the darts therefrom would arrive in a victim more widely spaced than at the source of their journey.

Slipping his weapon in his jacket pocket, 'Mopes' crossed to the refrigerator and from it took one of many self-freezing capsules, coated inside with dry ice and in themselves miniature refrigerators. These were the creation of the Chief. Within the capsules were about twenty glass-like tiny darts, actually nothing more than icicles, with rattlesnake venom frozen within them. The idea was deadly and brilliant. The ice slivers made the necessary punctures in the victim, and then promptly melted and released the venom into the bloodstream. 'Mopes' had never worked with so foolproof a weapon, and it suited his childish, brutal mind to blow darts with unerring accuracy.

Still humming to himself, capsule in his pocket alongside the blowpipe, he hurried upstairs again, wrapped himself up in his overcoat, drew his soft hat low down, and then left the mansion. In a matter of minutes he was driving swiftly down the main road that led eventually into the city. By early morning he was back again, and such was his nature he slept easily on the thought that one man and two women had died at his hands that night, horribly, in the destructive anguish of poison, before help could reach them.

The news of it reached Scotland Yard next day, from different sources. First, one of the women was found, then the man and, finally, the other woman. Because Grindberg had also died of snakebite, it seemed proper that these latest deaths from a similar cause should be laid at the door of Chief-Inspector Dawson.

'So we get deeper into the mire,' he commented bitterly, when he had looked through all three reports.

'I'd say exactly the opposite, sir,' Detective-Sergeant Harriday commented. 'We're relieved of one worry, surely? We know now that Grindberg's death from snakebite was coincidental and not deliberate. Otherwise, why were these other folk wiped out? They're totally unconnected with the Grindberg business, or indeed with anything at all out of the ordinary, if these reports are to be believed.'

'Coroner informed of each case,' Dawson mused. 'Let me see, now . . . ' He switched on the interphone and contacted Boyd Ensdale in the pathological division.

'Dawson here, sir. How about the three snakebite victims that have come in? Are you making out the reports on them for the coroner?'

'No,' came Ensdale's voice. 'Andrews is

doing that, but he asked for my opinion. It's the same as in the case of Grindberg. Genuine snakebite. Time that blasted serpent was found and killed, if you ask me.'

'Yes, indeed,' Dawson agreed. 'And thank you, sir.'

He switched off, and sat thinking for a moment.

'Somebody,' he said slowly, 'is being very clever. Tell me something, Bob: if you were deliberately faking snakebite wound, and had got rid of a possibly dangerous person by that method, what would you do to throw the police off the scent?'

Harriday reflected for a moment and then snapped his fingers.

'Polish off some independent victims to make it look as though the first snake attack was genuine.'

'Right! And that's what's happened here, I think. Which is all to the good. It shows we have our man worried — otherwise, he wouldn't go to such lengths.'

'And where are we?' Harriday sighed. 'Not a lead, not a clue. That warehouse certainly didn't tell us anything, and we can't pick up any information concerning the attack in the shop since nobody seems to have noticed what went on. The only concrete thing we have got is that 'Mopes' McCall is mixed up in it somewhere — but we've no way of finding out where he is.'

'Not at the moment,' Dawson agreed, pondering. 'Plainly, though, he isn't the brains behind all this. I think we need to look for a skilled scientist, and since there aren't so many in the country, we can do a bit of elimination and check on the movements of each one. Yes — that's it! I'll have lists of likely ones made out, and then I'll study them. In the meantime, since we haven't got anything else, you can go to work on another angle.'

'And what's that, sir?'

'Make a tour of every scrap metal foundry and yard you can dig up. He certainly won't pay top price for it, unless he's crazy, so that leads us to the junk and scrap yards. Find out what you can.'

'That I will, sir. And there's also

another angle. He can't make transmutations without some pretty costly up-to-date scientific apparatus. Maybe if we contacted the suppliers of generators, cathode ray tubes and general electronic equipment, we might get a lead.'

'Very good idea,' Dawson conceded. 'I'll tackle that over the phone, Bob. You get busy on the junk yards — now!'

Harriday wasted no more time. Neither, for that matter, did Dawson. But, as they realized, they had both started on a task that might take several days to complete, and in the interval there was nothing that could be done. Amongst other things, reports were gathered from the banks of modern coins suspected to be spurious — in various denominations — and they were submitted to Dawson for examination. So cleverly were they moulded, it was well nigh impossible to distinguish them from the real thing. Even the banks had been fooled. But the electron-microscope in the Yard's laboratory of physical research was not deceived. Side by side with genuine coins, the false ones revealed themselves by flaws in the lettering round the sides — flaws so minute that even an ordinary microscope could not spot them.

'Which,' Dawson declared, when Harriday enquired into progress, 'reveals that we're at work on a man, or number of men, who have considerable skill, and who probably relied on the fact that nobody would go to the length of using scientific instruments like the electron-microscope.'

'I don't suppose we would have done, sir, but for the fact that we found that phony sovereign on Grindberg. Everything has sprung from that.'

'Everything except a definite lead to take us to the heart of this business,' Dawson muttered. 'There's got to be a way, somehow . . .'

Meanwhile, at the mansion, 'Mopes' McCall was by no means in a good temper The provisions which the Chief had promised him had been duly delivered the night before — the night after he'd dealt with his three 'snakebite' victims — but he had only just discovered, in unpacking them, that the usual supply of cigarettes had been omitted. The obscenities that 'Mopes' then invoked upon the head of the provision merchant ought to have kited him stone dead — none of which altered the fact that 'Mopes' was without cigarettes, and boiling mad.

Finally, he looked at the clock. It was seven-thirty in the evening, dark outside, and too late for gaspers in this isolated spot — or was it? Suddenly, 'Mopes' remembered something and tugged his thick notebook from his shirt pocket, running a red sausage of a finger down a series of entries. When he came to 'Maudie Vincent, The Tobacco Shop', he grinned to himself.

'Why not?' he muttered, putting the notebook on the table and thinking. 'I ain't seen Maudie in three years. Be nice to see her, even though I mustn't let her recognize me. An' she's open till ten, or useta be.'

'Mopes' nodded promptly to himself. Cigarettes he had got to have, and he was prepared to take any risk to get them. It was unlikely the Chief would drop in; if he did, to hell with him! The provision merchant ought to do his job better. Then, as he got into his hat and overcoat and added dark glasses for good measure, he remembered something. He had no change — in fact no money at all. His last lot of wages he had 'blued' on the night of the murders, chiefly in public houses who defied the law by keeping open beyond the normal hours and he was not due for more wages until two more days had gone.

'Hell ruddy fire!' he muttered to himself, jamming his notebook into his overcoat pocket 'Wonder if Maudie would let me have 'em on tick? Nope, that wouldn't work, 'cos she wouldn't know it wus me.'

For the moment, his slow-moving brain was stuck. He felt again in his pockets, then, in some wonder, drew forth from his overcoat — the opposite pocket to where he had put his notebook — the double blowpipe and the capsule of icicle darts. He had quite forgotten to return them to the laboratory after his activity of two nights before. For a second or two, he wondered about having another snake orgy, since there were quite a number of darts still 'cold storaged' in the capsule.

'Hell — no!' he muttered, thrusting the stuff back in his pocket. 'Chief said only three. If more turned up, I might get me head punched . . . '

Abruptly, he stopped muttering. There, in the corner of the big room, lay the answer to his problem. The case of sovereigns, just as he and Nick had left it. He grinned. Maudie was pretty dumb, anyway, and she'd certainly never suspect a phony sovereign. Probably feel quite proud to have it. What was more, she could sell it at a considerable profit. It was a thought that made 'Mopes' feel good.

He crossed to the case, picked up one of the sovereigns, then set off in his car on his journey. It was a seven miles trip, but he made short work of it, and he knew there was not the least chance of his being apprehended. The night, and his trifling disguise, were sufficient guardians.

To his relief, Maudie Vincent's Tobacco Shop was open, just as it had been in the days when the blonde Maudie had been one of his many flames. Her main clientele was made up of seamen and dockhands, liable to need tobacco at all hours.

'Mopes' stopped the car at the end of the street and walked the remaining distance. Outside the shop, he peered in at the steamy window and could descry just a blurry vision of the blonde Maudie beyond. She looked pretty much the same as she'd ever done. Bit fatter, maybe, but that suited 'Mopes' perfectly. And there was nobody else in the shop.

He opened the door and entered, the old-fashioned bell clanging noisily over his head. Maudie looked up, somewhat surprised that, for once, it wasn't a seaman. The big fellow in the soft hat, faded Crombie overcoat and tinted glasses was — so she believed — a complete stranger to her.

'Sixty fags,' 'Mopes' said briefly, pointing to a display of his favoured brand, and watched her through the green fog of his glasses.

She nodded but did not speak, setting down three twenty packets on the counter. 'Mopes' fiddled around in his pocket for a moment and then dropped the sovereign in her hand. She looked at it in astonishment.

'Present for you,' he said, shrugging. 'I've no other money on me. It's worth maybe forty or fifty quid, but you can keep the difference.'

She looked at him. 'What's the idea, 'Mopes'?' she asked quietly.

He had half turned to go but now he turned back abruptly. Her eyes — they had wrinkles around them now — were searching his face intently.

'Huh?' he asked woodenly.

'Who are you trying to kid?' Maudie asked. 'I'd know that nutty-slack voice of yours anywhere. Even if it is years since I last heard it. That was when you proposed to me. Remember? And I never saw you again afterwards.'

'Yore crazy!' 'Mopes' said bluntly, and headed for the door, struggling to get the cigarettes in his pocket.

'Stop and turn round!' Maudie snapped, and there was something in her voice that made 'Mopes' obey. To his consternation, he beheld a .32 automatic held firmly in her right hand.

'What's the idea?' he demanded.

'Never mind. I've waited a long time for the off chance to get even with you for ditching me, 'Mopes', and maybe this is it. Are you so dumb that you don't know that ugly mug of yours has been splashed in the newspapers for killing that kid over at Grindberg's shop? Do you think I'm such a fool as to let you walk out, when I can turn you in? Come here!'

'Mopes' wandered slowly back to the counter, still struggling with his cigarette packets. He realized subconsciously that it was the blowpipe and capsule that were jamming them.

'That's a nice bit of hardware you've got there,' he commented, eyeing the gun.

'Yes — and it's licensed. I need protection sometimes against the sort of characters there are around here.'

'Mopes' was silent, his brain working slowly — and, as usual it tended towards homicide. He was wondering how this faded piece had ever attracted him. But then, she hadn't been so faded when he'd last seen her

'You're mixed up in phony sovereigns, too,' she went on, her eyes merciless. 'That's been in the papers. Don't you ever read 'em?'

'Sure I do. You're a smart girl, Maudie — smarter than I thought.'

'I'm certainly not so dumb I'm taking a phony sovereign and letting you get out of here. The next customer who comes in is going to the police while I pin you — just as I'm doing now.'

'Mopes' sighed, tugged out the jammed cigarette packets, and tossed them on the counter. Then he felt in his other pocket.

'Get your hand outa there!' Maudie commanded.

'All right, don't get all fidgety. No harm in crossing your perishin' name off me list, is there?'

'Mopes' brought his fat notebook in sight, flipped the pages and then laboriously tugged out a pencil stump and lined through Maudie's name. She watched sourly.

'That bulgin' book full of girl friends?

104

Must be the hell of a lot of 'em!'

'Mopes' shrugged — then, with a sudden lightning action, he flashed the book out of his hand and straight into Maudie's face. Inevitably, she jolted back and, in that instant, 'Mopes' smashed his right straight to her jaw, knocking her out completely. It was practically a repetition of the assault on Betty Lathom, except that in this case, Maudie was still living. Her heaving bosom showed it clearly.

'Mopes' glanced about him and then stuffed the cigarettes into the now empty pocket where the notebook had been. The notebook itself he couldn't spot at the moment; it could wait a few seconds, anyway; probably it was behind the counter. He had something more important to concentrate upon.

Again he looked about him; then, quickly, he took out his blowpipe and capsule. In a matter of seconds he had fitted two of the venomous darts in position and took careful aim. With a soft 'phut' they lauded in the soft flesh of Maudie's upper arm, drawing two tiny spots of blood. She stirred slightly in unconsciousness.

'Mopes' grinned and thrust the capsule and blowpipe back in his pocket; then he turned to look for his fallen notebook. It seemed to have gone under the . . . Then the doorbell clanged as a customer entered. He gulped and began to sweat. At the moment, his stooping position behind the counter hid him. He shuffled quickly on all fours, reaching the back regions just as a blue-jerseyed seaman banged on the counter for attention.

'Maudie! Maudie! Come out, wherever you are!'

'Mopes', thinking of nothing but imminent danger to himself, fled through the dim little kitchen and escaped by the back door. In twenty seconds flat, he had pelted down the nearest alleyway to his car. He jumped in and was in the midst of the London traffic before he remembered he had never recovered his notebook. After dully thinking out the situation, he arrived at the conclusion that it didn't matter much, anyway. The book did not contain his name — only the names of girl friends he'd had, questionable jokes, and odd statements that made sense only to himself. And Maudie was done for, anyway, and wouldn't be able to speak. There was, of course, the phony sovereign, which Maudie had put on the counter . . . What the hell did any of it matter, anyway? He drove on, reasonably sure that all was well.

Back at Maudie's, however, things were happening. Deckhand Swanson, the customer whom 'Mopes' had glimpsed entering, did not take above thirty seconds to discover the sprawled body of Maudie and the peculiar puncture wound on her arm. He did not know what it signified, but he did know she was out cold. In ten minutes, an ambulance was rushing her to the general hospital. Once there, the authorities informed the Yard that a new snake victim had been brought in. Chief-Inspector Dawson and Harriday, both prepared for just such a contingency, were whipped from their respective homes to sudden duty.

In an hour, Maudie's place had been photographed, fingerprinted and generally combed out. With this done, Dawson remained behind, tossing the phony sovereign slowly up and down in his palm as he stood thinking.

'We've got something, Bob,' he said finally. 'No snake ever did come into here — except a human one. That woman had only just been bitten about fifteen minutes earlier, according to the latest report from the hospital. That means the snake would still be here, and it isn't. That satisfies me that the snake-biting business is brilliant murder . . . ' Dawson turned and took up the notebook from the counter. Since it had already been inspected and photographed for finger-prints, he could handle it freely.

'Whoever owns this has a mind like a cesspool,' he said, studying some of the pages. 'In fact, just the kind of mind to contemplate murder without a single qualm. Okay, we've done all we can here. Let's get to the hospital now.'

Leaving a police constable in charge, and advising the deckhand, who was waiting in a back room, that he might be required later, Dawson and Harriday wasted no time in getting to the hospital.

Eventually, they were joined in an anteroom by a white-coated surgeon.

'How is she?' Dawson asked quickly.

'Still unconscious. We've given her an antidote serum but, so far, it hasn't reacted. Apparently, she's been very badly bitten. Quite frankly, Inspector, snake-bite is a little out of our territory. It's a specialist's job, and I can't be sure where to locate one.'

'At all costs, that woman has got to be revived,' the Chief-Inspector said curtly. 'Even if only for long enough to tell us what happened. Maybe I can help. Where's the nearest phone?'

The surgeon led the way out of the anteroom and to the telephone in an adjoining office. Dawson picked up the instrument quickly, and rang a Whitehall number.

'That you, Bedford? Dawson speaking. Get in touch with Mr. Ensdale immediately and have him ring me back here. He'll probably be at home, and I don't know his private number. Hurry it up: it's urgent.'

This done. Dawson put the instrument

down again and began to pace slowly. The surgeon excused himself and returned a few minutes afterwards with a shake of his head.

'No recovery yet,' he announced. 'Who's Ensdale, anyway? Think he can do something? I never heard of him.'

'That's not very surprising. He's exclusive to the Yard, in the pathology and scientific branch. Knows a lot about snakebite; investigated every victim so far — excuse me.'

Dawson picked up the phone as it shrilled. Boyd Ensdale's voice came from the other end of the wire.

'Dawson here, Mr. Ensdale. I need your help — and quickly. There's a snakebite victim here, but she isn't dead yet. She needs expert help, correct serum administration and all the rest of it. At all costs she must be revived.'

'Whereabouts are you?'

'East London General Hospital.'

'Okay. I'll come. Be as quick as I can.'

'Thanks.' Dawson put down the phone and looked relieved. 'He's coming; everything depends on whether he'll be in time.'

So, for all those concerned, there descended a deep uncertainty until Ensdale arrived — which was twenty minutes later. Though it was the early hours of the morning by now, he looked fresh and alert, carrying with him a significant looking black bag. Conducted by the surgeon to the room where the stricken Maudie was lying, Dawson and Harriday found themselves forced to wait in the anteroom once again. At length Ensdale reappeared.

'She's conscious,' he said briefly, 'and I think she'll live, too.'

'Can I talk to her?' Dawson demanded.

Ensdale seemed to hesitate for a second, then he gave a nod.

'Yes, go ahead. I'll come with you.'

Conducted to the side of Maudie's bed, Dawson sat down and studied her intently. She was definitely conscious again, and fully comprehensive of her surroundings as well.

'I'm a police officer, Miss Vincent,' Dawson displayed his warrant card. 'I suppose you know what's been happening? That you were bitten by a snake?'

'So I'm told,' she assented. 'I remember being hit by one, but not being bitten.'

'Meaning what, exactly?' Dawson said, tensing forward sharply.

'Meaning that somebody you'd dearly love to lock up came into my shop this evening — 'Mopes' McCall. I used to know him in the old days and I think he was trying to renew the acquaintance. He tried to pass a phony sovereign, but I held him to the point of my gun. He threw a fat notebook at me, hit me in the jaw, and I passed out. I don't remember anything more.'

'You don't remember any snake?' Dawson asked deliberately.

'No. Maybe 'Mopes' could tell you something about that if you can catch him . . . hell!' Maudie broke off, wincing. 'My arm's aching fit to drop off.'

'Just take it easy, Miss Vincent,' Dawson murmured 'and thanks for telling me what you have.'

Getting up, he jerked his head to Ensdale and Harriday and led the way back to the anteroom.

'The only explanation is that she must

have been unconscious from the blow in the jaw when the snakebite act took place,' he said, turning from closing the door. 'Which is a damnable pity. I felt sure we'd learn for certain this time that the snakebites are artificial.'

'I think you're up the wrong tree there, Dawson,' Ensdale said. 'This woman's wound is identical to all those inflicted on the other victims and I still maintain it is genuine snakebite.'

'Then how did that snake vanish so quickly? I'm no expert, but I'll swear no snake would move that fast.'

'It could, you know,' Ensdale said. 'Rattlers move very fast on occasions, particularly when they hear footsteps. Anyhow,' he added, shrugging, 'I've done all I can and, as near as I can tell you, Miss Vincent will probably recover completely. If you need me again, just let me know.'

'Yes.' Dawson looked preoccupied. 'Thanks, sir. You've been invaluable.'

Ensdale took his departure and for several minutes, Dawson remained nearly motionless, following a chain of reasoning; then, at length, he caught Harriday's questioning eyes. The Detective-Sergeant was looking very tired and very disappointed.

'All that sweat for nothing sir, from the looks of it.'

'Not entirely Bob — not entirely. I'll grant you that we're hamstrung on the snake angle, but we've got another one. A mighty good one, too! I mean the notebook, of course.'

'Yes?' Harriday's brow creased as he tried to see the point.

'We know,' Dawson continued deliberately, 'that 'Mope' McCall has one weak point — women. Any woman on earth can make a sucker out of him. That much is in his own case history at the records department. Now, suppose a highly delectable young woman were to insert an advertisement in the personal column of a daily newspaper, saying she had his notebook and wanted to return it to him. What then?'

'He mightn't read that particular paper,' Harriday pointed out stolidly.

'You're a good policeman Bob, but you've no imagination,' Dawson said patiently. 'The ad would be in every worthwhile daily paper, morning and evening and I'm darned sure 'Mopes' must read one or other of them in order to keep in touch with the outer world. On the other hand, he may rely on television or radio. If he does, we'll have to contrive something that way, but first, let's try the newspapers.'

'He might bite,' Harriday admitted dubiously, 'but on the other hand, I can't see that there is anything incriminating enough in that notebook for him to take a risk to get it back. Certainly, we've got nothing out of it.'

'We're trying the psychological angle,' Dawson explained. 'I've never yet known it to fail, especially with the vain type of criminal such as 'Mopes.' The advertisement must be well thought out. It's got to bring him out of his lair. The notebook is not valuable to us, but it will be to him, because it lists the addresses and phone numbers of dozens of girls with whom he evidently had contact before getting jailed. He'll try and get it back — even more so if he learns what a bright young thing has discovered it.'

'How will he know that? The advertisement won't say so.'

'Not to begin with. I'll show you later what happens. He might even be dense enough to give away his address and, if so, the thing's easy. Once nail 'Mopes', and we'll nail everybody including the brains behind this counterfeiting, snake-biting racket.'

'You're not suggesting Maudie Vincent as the delectable one, surely?' Harriday asked, in surprise. 'All due respect to her, but her charm's had it, sir.'

'I'm thinking of Gwenda Blane,' Dawson mused. 'She's helped us before, and will again, I'm sure — for a consideration. Pretty as they make 'em, and as tough as they come. A very curvaceous sprat to catch a mighty big whale, Bob.'

5

By mid-morning, Chief-Inspector Dawson had the 'Personal' advertisement framed in words that satisfied him, and it was immediately forwarded to every daily of repute. The possibility of an evening paper was one that Dawson ruled out as less likely to offer results. The other point he dealt with was suppression of all information concerning Maudie Vincent — at least, for the time being. Plainly, if 'Mopes' read that she had recovered, he would tie it up with the advertisement and probably that she herself was the possessor of his note-book; which, in itself, would be enough to prevent him walking into the trap. Depending on how matters were shaping, Dawson was prepared to circulate a false report concerning Maudie's death if necessary.

His next move was to have Gwenda Blane come over to the Yard and, as on other occasions, she did so the moment she was free — around lunchtime.

Gwenda was a somewhat remarkable girl — artist's model, cover girl, swimsuit mannequin, and a chorine on occasion. She had beauty, brains and single blessedness and meant to keep all three. Above all things, she had plenty of courage and, more than once, had hired herself out as 'bait' for the Yard when they needed a girl of unusual attractiveness and plenty of intelligence.

'Whether this assignment will prove dangerous or not I can't say at this stage, Gwen,' Dawson explained in a frank statement. 'You can hear the details and then take it or leave it. In any case, we're obliged to you for coming along.'

The girl, fake fur-coated and smiling in that particularly icy way she had, merely shrugged.

'I know you Yard men occasionally borrow your sisters and sweethearts to help you out in a case, so why am I different from them? Anything for a change. But what's it all about?'

'Spurious sovereigns, a dull-witted killer, and maybe a brilliant and completely ruthless scientist.'

'Spurious sovereigns? Sounds like the Grindberg business to me.'

'It is. We can't use a policewoman for this job, either — they automatically give themselves away to those criminal types accustomed to them. What we're trying to do is drag a woman-crazy killer into the open. Once we've got him we hope to have the whole racket broken wide open. He'll talk before we're through with him.'

'Who is he?' Gwenda asked.

' 'Mopes' McCall. Do I need to say more, or are you up on your newspapers?'

The girl smiled faintly. 'I've read about him, Inspector, and he seems to be a charming personality. Well, what do I have to do?'

'Read this first.' And Dawson pushed across a copy of the advertisement he had worked out. Gwenda took it in a delicately manicured hand and read out the words:

'Why mope about looking for your notebook? I'm worth dating up, too. Young, pretty, and willing. If you want me and the notebook, contact . . . ' Gwenda frowned slightly as she saw the telephone number that concluded the advertisement. 'Thanks for the build-up,' she murmured, as she handed the paper back. 'But where is that telephone number? It certainly isn't my mine.'

'It's the phone number of a flat you will occupy while working for us. Been used before on other jobs, but 'Mopes' won't know that. Go there, live there, and wait there. The moment you hear anything, inform me immediately. Mind you, I don't know that this dimwit 'Mopes' will even fall for the ad., or even see it — but we're hoping he will. Well, still with us?'

'Certainly, provided I'm allowed to retain my .32 automatic. I don't feel safe otherwise. It's licensed and everything.'

'Technically, you're against the law,' Dawson replied, 'but we'll let that pass for the moment. Now, here's the address of the flat. You can use your own name; it won't signify.'

Dawson scribbled it out and handed it over. 'You can go in the moment you're ready, and this is the key.'

'Kensington, eh? Swank part thereof. Well, thanks very much. How long do you suppose the job will take? I'm contracted a fortnight hence for a French stage show.'

'We'll get results before then, Gwen, or else release you. Meantime, here's your cheque. Half now, half when we finish, based on the same terms as other occasions. Fair enough?'

'Fair enough,' Gwenda smiled, rising and shaking hands. 'I'll be on to you the moment anything happens in this business.'

Dawson saw her to the door and then turned to behold Harriday also looking at the door, somewhat in regret.

'Pity I don't fit into that part of the assignment, too sir,' he sighed. 'Of all the blondes I ever did see, she really . . . '

'Keep your mind on your work,' Dawson growled, 'and don't be too sure you won't be mixed up with Gwenda before we're finished. That's up to 'Mopes'.' Dawson settled down at his desk and looked through the reports. 'Nothing on the scrap iron dealers yet, I see, Bob.'

'Afraid not, sir, though I've still a good few to visit.'

'All right; keep on doing that. Not that I've any room to talk, either. I haven't located anything significant from the manufacturers of electronic equipment and similar gadgets. Our mastermind is keeping up to standard as far as subtlety is concerned. Maybe he's been ordering separate pieces from different firms to avoid buying a lot of stuff in one place.'

'Could be,' Harriday sighed, reaching for his coat. 'And, incidentally, sir . . . '

'Yes?' Dawson waited.

'I've been doing a bit of thinking on my own about this snakebite business. If each snakebite is a fake, how come that so brilliant a pathologist as Mr. Ensdale can't detect it?'

'I've wondered about that, too,' Dawson murmured. 'Very cunning snakebite imitation. That's the only answer . . . I suppose . . . '

Harriday reflected, hesitated over something, and then changed his mind.

'I'll carry on with the scrap iron,' he said, and went on his way. Dawson turned back to his notes, particularly one that he had made himself to the effect that a genuine snakebite would show traces of saliva. He considered it for a moment or two, and then switched on the interphone.

'Dr. Andrews?' he asked, after a moment.

'Right here, Inspector. Can I help you?'

'Perhaps. I'm still fretting over those snakebites. You examined the victims to commence with, and Mr. Ensdale confirmed your reports. Maybe you can tell me something. In the case of the victims you examined, did you find any traces of saliva in the snakebite wound — as you certainly would from a genuine bite?'

'None at all. Puzzling thing, I know — but there it is.'

'Then why did you state positively that the wounds were caused by a snake? Why not admit the possibility of a fake?'

Dr. Andrews' reply was dryly pedantic.

'I'm not concerned with possibilities, Inspector; that's your job. I merely state the medical evidence. I said genuine snakebites because I couldn't think of anything likely to duplicate them so completely.'

'I see. But, in no case, was there a trace of snake saliva?'

'None.'

'Much obliged.' Dawson switched off, his sharp eyes narrowed over a thought. Then the jarring of the telephone disturbed him again.

'Dawson here,' he announced.

'*Daily Monarch*, Inspector. We've had a hospital report that Maudie Vincent died an hour ago. Are we allowed to print that, along with the story of what was the cause of her death?'

'Died?' Dawson repeated, astonished. 'But the last I heard of her, she was making good progress.'

'So we thought. Apparently Mr. Ensdale, of your scientific squad, called in to see how she was going on, found her as good as expected, and then left. But an hour ago she died. Some kind of relapse from the snake poison.'

'I see.' Dawson thought for a moment. 'Yes, print the story, by all means, but suppress all details concerning the Yard. You can say simply that she was killed by a snake in her shop last night.'

'But there's more to it than that, Inspector! Have a heart! What about the phony sovereign on the counter, and that notebook you found on the floor . . . '

'Suppress all that. That's an order! You'll not be scooped, because the same order will go to the entire press. When anything big breaks — as it must before long — I'll see you get everything.'

'Okay.'

Dawson put the telephone down, his eyes hard. Then he checked with the hospital to make certain — but there was no doubt about it. Maudie Vincent had suffered a relapse and died. Not even a question of an inquest being held up for further enquiry. It would be a verdict of 'death from misadventure'.

In the meantime, 'Mopes' McCall was entirely satisfied with himself. The morning newspaper, delivered religiously by the village's only newsagent, and paid for by the Chief in some roundabout manner best known to himself, did not splash the fate of Maudie Vincent. It merely made a passing reference to the fact — in an obscure corner — that she had been bitten by a snake and taken to hospital in a coma. Nothing more.

'And coma is the overture to death,' 'Mopes' told himself, between mouthfuls of a late breakfast. 'Which makes me safe. She'll pass out before she can say anything — if she hasn't passed out already.'

Finding no other information, he had to content himself until mid-morning radio and television news bulletins — but no reference at all was made to Maudie Vincent, doubtless because she was not important enough in the general scheme of things. Nor was there any news in the early evening bulletins, either.

Disgusted and vaguely uncertain, in spite of himself, 'Mopes' settled down for an evening watching television and listening to the radio but, towards seven-thirty, his hermitage was interrupted by the arrival of the Chief. Grim-faced, he came slowly into the room, drawing off his gloves.

'Well, what's the explanation?' he asked coldly, as 'Mopes' struggled from the chesterfield and began to straighten his tie.

'Explanation, Chief? Oh, you mean I've

got the television too loud again . . . '

'I mean the snakebite which laid out Maudie Vincent. And put that damned thing off!'

'Mopes' obeyed, sweating a little. There was a diabolical expression on the Chief's face that made him wish his hand were holding a loaded gun.

'Maudie Vincent?' 'Mopes' enquired vaguely. 'Did you say snakebite? I — I don't get it. Was she one of those I finished off the other night, like you told me?'

The Chief sat down. 'I'll give you sixty seconds, 'Mopes'. Why did you dare to 'snakebite' that woman without my orders? Why did you leave a false sovereign where everybody could see it?'

'False sovereign? I ain't seen nothing in the papers about a false sovereign . . . ' 'Mopes' narrowed his eyes.

'You have only one paper here: I see nearly all of them in my capacity. One states distinctly that a false sovereign was left on the counter of the tobacco shop. What did you do it for, 'Mopes'?'

'Mopes' breathed hard, staring at the

.38 that had now appeared in the Chief's hand. He knew that if he did not speak, his number was definitely up.

'I went for fags,' he blurted out. 'I had to. Only place I could think of. You didn't let me have any in the grocery order — else the feller didn't send 'em. Anyway, I chose Maudie Vincent 'cos I useta know her long ago. I went disguised an' I didn't mean to snakebite her. She recognized me in spite of everything, an' to save things, I let her have it. I had to get out quick 'cos of a customer, an' I musta left the sovereign on the counter.'

'Why didn't you use your own money?'

'I had none. I used it up the other night.'

The gun lowered and finally disappeared. 'All right. I believe that, 'Mopes', because you're too dumb to invent so consecutive a story on the spur of the moment. I'm not going to do anything to you, because as far as I can tell, the police have not got anything out of the business. Plenty of suspicion, but nothing definite. What I am going to do is warn you.'

''bout what?'

'Something may be attempted. You left your fingerprints in that shop, and the police will know they're yours. They will also know that if they can grab you, you can give everything away. So, to preserve yourself, and the rest of us, ignore any attempt that may be made to contact you. Understand?'

'Uh-huh.'

'All right. And don't try anything funny again, or I'll finish you for good. And don't think, either, that you're invaluable to me. A day will come when I won't need you any more and, when it does, I'll remember that you took far too much on your own shoulders.'

Without saying any more the Chief departed. 'Mopes' grimaced, spat into the glowing fire and then resumed his sprawl on the chesterfield. But his mind very soon reverted to the Chief's last words.

'A day'll come, will it?' 'Mopes' muttered. 'We'll damned well see about that! If he can spring something on me just whenever he feels like it, I can also spring something on 'im — an' I will. Just give me the chance, that's all.'

He got up again, switched on the television, and left it on until midnight. Then he ate as large a supper as he could find and went to bed. Next morning, the newspaper had a front page statement to the effect that Maudie Vincent, victim number five to succumb to a mysterious rattlesnake, had died. The police had no reason to suspect foul play, though they were puzzled by the spurious sovereign. Nothing about him, nothing about his notebook having been found. He grinned widely to himself.

'So long, Maudie!' he exclaimed, raising his coffee cup. 'Happy landings . . .'

For him, the matter of Maudie Vincent was literally dead and done with. He browsed through the news of the latest assaults and robberies, surveyed the pictures of a new batch of debutantes, and then looked at the 'Deaths' to see if anybody he knew had kicked the bucket. It was this survey that automatically led him to the 'Personal' column, immediately below. And it was the word 'mope' that caught his eye.

' 'Why mope about looking for your

notebook?' ' he repeated slowly. ' 'I'm worth dating up, too. Young, pretty and willing. If you want me and the notebook, contact . . . ' ' The telephone number concluded the entry.

He stopped eating and read the advertisement right through again. Notebook? Mope? Was somebody trying to contact him without giving anything away? It took him a long time to realize that this was the general idea. It could only mean that another customer had found his notebook, or somehow got hold of it. Maybe that explained why the police had not mentioned it.

'Hellfire!' 'Mopes' exclaimed finally, as at last he worked things out. 'I do believe it is meant for me! Who's she say she is? Young, pretty and willing . . . Mmm — could be me all right. She musta read that blasted notebook to know about the dating up. Whoever she is, she's smart, or she wouldn't ha' put in an ad. like that! Just about my measure, I'd say.'

'Mopes' swallowed some more coffee before he was pervaded with the final conviction that the ad. did apply to him.

There drifted across his mind a memory of the Chief's warning: and, just as quickly, he discarded it. Here was a young, pretty woman — if she was to be believed — and she had somehow found the notebook and wanted to hand it back. It certainly couldn't be Maudie, because she was dead.

'Okay — what have I gotta lose?' 'Mopes' murmured. 'Only thing is to figure out how to get in touch without givin' anythin' away.'

The Chief had not trusted him with a telephone in the house. His first impulse was to dash out there and then to a phone box; then he checked himself. He had never appeared outside by day for any length of time, except in the car and, since the phone box was only a hundred yards down the road, there was no sense in getting out the car for that — or was there? Then 'Mopes' remembered something else, and cursed. He had no money. Only those blasted spurious sovereigns, until he received his next wage packet.

'Reverse the charge, you dope!' he told himself; then he shook his head. That wouldn't do, either. The operator would want his name. No reason why he must give his own name, though. Finally, he made his decision. He would use the car and phone immediately. This was urgent.

Accordingly, ten minutes later — disguised with his dark glasses as usual — he had reached the telephone booth, asked for the number given in the paper, and given his name as Johnson, so the charge could be reversed. At length, there floated to him a sweetly feminine voice.

'Hello? I'm allowing you to reverse the charge because I think I know why you have rung up.'

'It's about the advertisement,' 'Mopes' said, picturing the delectable vision at the other end of the wire.

'So I thought. What did the operator say your name is? Mr. Johnson?'

'That's it, Miss. Bobby Johnson. What do I do to pick up the notebook?'

'Well, now . . . I'd better think about that. It's rather important, isn't it? Do you know where I found it?'

'I — I c'n guess,' 'Mopes' answered uneasily.

'I found it in Maudie Vincent's Tobacco Shop. Just how I found it, I'll tell you later. It could do you an awful lot of harm if the police got it, couldn't it?'

'Mebbe.'

'Tell you what you do,' Gwenda Blane said, after an interval. 'Ring me back here in ten minutes and, by then, I'll have thought out some arrangement.'

'Can't you fix something now?' 'Mopes' demanded. 'I've precious little time to spare.'

'I know, but we want things to be absolutely safe, don't we? I'm taking a risk, and so are you. I must work out some kind of plan. Ring me back — ten minutes from now.'

'Can I reverse the charge — ? I'm short of change.'

'Certainly, if you wish. 'Bye for now.'

The line clicked and 'Mopes' put down the phone. He was not sure whether he liked the set-up or not. Still, nothing had been done so far that could give him away. It was the ten minutes wait he didn't feel comfortable about. Anything could happen in that time. Okay — if it did, he'd be ready for it. So he remained

134

in the phone box, the car just within sight, and kept his eyes open for anything unusual.

Meantime, Gwen was speaking to Dawson at the Yard. It did not take her above a few seconds to give the details. 'So — what do I do now?' she asked.

'Ask him to your flat,' Dawson replied promptly. 'By every means you know, get him to talk. That's the main thing.'

'You'll be around somewhere, won't you?' Gwenda asked anxiously. 'I'm panicky of having a gorilla like that locked up with me.'

'We'll certainly keep watch,' Dawson answered, 'but we're not going to make any actual arrest until 'Mopes' has told everything he knows. For us to make him talk — since we're limited in this country as to how far we can go in that direction — may be difficult, but you can do it if you play the game right. Once we have all the information we want, we'll be busy. That drawing room of yours is wired up, by the way, and your entire conversation will be recorded by an operator in a room two blocks away. Good luck, and keep us posted. We'll know how you're fixed, by the operator being in constant touch with us here. Fix your appointment for seven tonight, if you can.'

She rang off and, in the drawing room of her temporary flat, looked about her in surprise, wondering where the microphone might be. She even looked right at it, but was not aware of it, since it comprised the rosette in the ceiling, from which depended the electric light flex. Then the phone was ringing again and 'Mopes' was at the other end.

'Johnson 'ere,' he said briefly. 'Made up your mind, sweetheart?'

'Yes, Mr. Johnson — I've made up my mind. You be here tonight at seven o'clock, and you shall have your notebook. Maybe we'll have a little chat, too, eh? You sound the rugged type of man that I admire.'

'Mopes' metaphorically preened himself. 'That will suit me fine, Miss — er — what's the name, by the way?'

'Gwenda Blane. I'm an artist's model. The address is eleven, Caradoc Mansions, Kensington. Two floors up you'll find me.'

'I'll be lookin' forward to it,' 'Mopes' promised, and rang off.

For the rest of the day, he was preparing himself for the evening, titivating his appearance for one thing — which was about as useful as painting an old car ready for the scrap-heap — and removing marks from his clothing with a bottle of solvent. He once or twice had the presentiment that he was walking into a trap and, if so, was prepared to shoot his way out of it with the automatic he carried in a shoulder holster. On the other hand, the whole thing might be genuine, and he had no intention of missing an evening with an artist's model for anybody. And if the Chief came . . . ? Well — er — oh, to Hades with the Chief!

Promptly at six-fifteen, as darkness was fast closing in, 'Mopes' set off in the car. He drove as far as a garage on the west side of the city and finished the journey on foot. He had no intention of giving any coppers the chance of noting the car, taking its number, and then trailing him back to the mansion.

So, exactly at seven, he knocked on the

door of Flat 11 in the Caradoc Mansions edifice, and almost immediately the girl herself opened it. 'Mopes' gave a gulp and adjusted his tinted glasses. He had been prepared for a girl worth looking at, but hardly for the feminine pulchritude that stood just within the softly lighted, scented drawing room.

'Mr. Johnson?' she asked softly.

'Yep — I'm Johnson.' 'Mopes' clumsily pulled off his hat. He was glad the tinted glasses disguised the fact that he was staring hard at Gwenda. Anyway, he just couldn't help it. She was wearing a 'lo-and-behold' evening gown of cherry taffeta, so low, indeed, off the shoulder that even 'Mopes' was surprised. Her shoulders and arms, softly rounded, were matt white, and her definitely pretty face was exquisitely made up. Crowning it all was the honey-colored hair, gently controlled by a golden clasp.

'Well, come in,' she invited, smiling. 'I don't suppose, judging from your notebook, that you're the kind of man who believes in ethics. Like us being alone here, for instance?'

'Mopes' got one look from those blue eyes and did not waste any more time. He followed the bare-backed, curvacious Gwenda into the room and closed the door behind him. He tossed down his hat and then removed his tinted glasses.

'Why, I do believe you're . . . 'Mopes' McCall!' the girl said slowly, staring at him. 'I never thought of that possibility.'

'Does it matter?' he asked curtly.

'Not a bit. Might make things more exciting, in fact. I've often wondered what it might be like to come face to face with a killer.'

Gwenda settled herself on the chester-field, her arm laid along its back.

'Okay, if you want to be blunt about it,' 'Mopes' growled. 'What about me note-book? Let me have that, an' I'll be on my way.'

'So soon?' Gwenda looked surprised. 'But surely you have time to talk? Time for a drink?'

'Well, I . . . '

Without giving him time to answer, Gwenda got up again and swept, with a faint rustling sound, to a cocktail cabinet.

After a moment or two, she returned to his side with drinks in her hands.

'Now, Mr. McCall — sit down and make yourself comfortable. I want to talk to you.'

'Oh, y'do?' 'Mopes' sat on the chesterfield, since she indicated it; then, with a waft of perfume, she reclined beside him.

'To us,' she said, raising her drink.

'Mopes' swallowed his drink at a gulp and then sat looking at her, trying to decide what was the matter with him. Normally, he dealt with women exactly as he chose, yet now he was side by side with one of the most beautiful girls he had ever seen, he didn't know what to do about it. She was literally throwing herself at him, and he wasn't sure of himself.

'You're not at all what I expected,' she said, taking his empty glass and setting it down with her own on the occasional table. 'A ruthless killer, an escaped convict, a man responsible for faked sovereigns — and you sit there like a little boy waiting for Sunday School to start.'

'How'd you know all about me?' he snapped.

'The newspapers, of course. That face of yours has been pretty well advertised, believe me. But don't think I've any ideas about turning you over to the police . . .'

'You'd better not try!'

'Supposing I did? What would you do?'

'Blot you out, same as 'appened to Maudie Vincent.' Gwenda's eyebrows rose. 'Maudie Vincent? But I thought the papers said she died of a snake-bite wound, didn't they?'

'Mebbe she did.' 'Mopes' compressed his thick lips, realizing he had already said too much. To his relief, Gwenda did not pursue the problem of Maudie, but she still asked very awkward questions, just the same.

'Wouldn't you rather turn yourself in, Mr. McCall, than keep dodging, the police? Don't you find it tough going?'

'Nope. I'm well cared for.'

'Then you've got a wife — or friends?'

'I'm not sayin' — but I know what I'm doin'. Now look, baby — let's get to business. Where's my notebook?'

'No hurry,' Gwenda said lazily, sprawling back on the chesterfield. 'It isn't often

I have a man of your type to talk to, and I mean to take advantage of it. What are you so jumpy about? You're quite safe here.'

'I'm not so sure about that. I don't feel safe when I'm not on me home ground. Now, if you wus at my place, where I'm stayin', it'd be different. I've always said the place needs a woman in it to brighten it up.'

'Whereabouts is it?'

'Out in the country. Safer than here.' 'Mopes' hesitated and then plunged. 'I could take you straight to it in me car. Then, if it's fun you want, we could really have it.'

Gwenda smiled wryly. 'I'm not that crazy, Mr. McCall — at least, not at the moment. Maybe, if I need a tough boy friend, I'll call on you some time. What's the address?'

'Never mind. The only way you'll ever get to my place is for me to take you. Now get that notebook, will you, and let me get outa here.'

'Aren't you interested in knowing how I found it?'

'Not particularly — but you can tell me, if it makes you any happier.'

'I walked into Maudie's shop just as a deck-hand was coming out. I went in for cigarettes and, to my surprise, this chap told me to keep an eye on the body while he phoned the police. I looked around and saw Maudie on the floor, and your notebook near her. I picked it up and read parts of it, then I decided I'd keep it instead of handing it over to the police.'

'Why?' 'Mopes' demanded suspiciously. 'What made you so keen on protectin' me?'

'I didn't know it was you. Could have been anybody. I rather fancied meeting the man who'd written some of the stuff in that book.'

'Uh-huh. Well, I'll take it, if you don't mind.'

Gwenda sighed. 'All right. Sure you won't have another drink?'

'Nope. Just give me the book and I'll blow.'

Gwenda gave it up. It was no use trying any more, as far as she could see. 'Mopes' was completely ill at ease and nothing of her devising could overcome that. Rising, she went to the bureau, withdrew the notebook from it, and came across with it.

'Don't I get anything for saving you?' she asked.

'Not here you don't!' 'Mopes' snatched it from her. 'I keep on telling you, baby, I'm not comfortable away from me home ground. Mebbe you'll change your mind and come out to my place? You'll be safe enough.'

'That,' Gwenda murmured, 'is a matter of opinion. Just the same, I'll give it some thought. The boys I know are pretty boring.'

'Then make up your mind quick. The car's waitin', and . . . '

'I'm not coming on the spur of the moment, Mr. McCall. I want to think it out first. You can ring me tomorrow if you like, and I'll see how I feel by then.'

'Okay.' 'Mopes' pig eyes gleamed momentarily. 'You an' me could have one hell of a time . . . I'll ring tomorrow mornin'. 'Bye for now.'

He snatched up his hat with one hand

and jammed his tinted glasses on his nose with the other. Then he was gone and, the instant the door closed, Gwenda lifted the telephone.

She waited impatiently as the line buzzed; then, at last, Dawson was on the line.

'Yes, Gwenda — what news?' he asked eagerly.

'Nothing much — and you'll hear what went on when you get the recording. I've rung you to see if you can track 'Mopes' down. He's got a car, and . . . '

'You don't have to worry over that. 'Mopes' is being watched. He was seen to enter your apartment building and, naturally, he'll be trailed as he leaves.'

'Oh well, that's all right. He left a few minutes ago. When you've heard the recording, Inspector, let me know what I must do next. As you'll find, I've left the door ajar — and, if helps matters, I'll walk into the lion's den.'

'I'll ring you back,' Dawson promised. 'They'll be bringing the recording in any time now.'

6

Chief-Inspector Dawson did not come to any snap decision when he heard the recording played through.

The first time, he just listened; the second time, he made notes; and the third time, he had Harriday and Boyd Ensdale listen, also. Indeed, getting wind of what was transpiring, Ensdale insisted on being present to keep track of events. Apparently the mystery of the snakebites was still worrying him.

'Well, there it is,' Dawson said finally. Then he glanced at the clock, which registered ten minutes past midnight. 'And I hope Gwenda Blane isn't sitting up waiting for me to ring her. I've still to think out what has to be done.'

'I don't see why she can't be dispensed with,' Harriday commented, stifling a yawn. 'She did all she could, to judge from that recording, but obviously 'Mopes' was too cagey. We didn't get a thing out of it.'

'Except his admission that he finished Maudie Vincent,' Dawson pointed out. 'That in turn proves what I've believed all along — that the snake-bites are deliberately created.'

'Begins to look like it, in the face of that,' Ensdale admitted, frowning. 'Damned clever faking, though.'

'Why do we have to waste any more time?' Harriday asked, spreading his hands. 'The boys have traced 'Mopes' to that old mansion, so we know exactly where he is. Let's go and get him!'

'And, when we do, what happens to the rest of the counterfeiters and murderers?' Dawson demanded. 'They'll vanish utterly when they know what's happened — as they will, thanks to the press. Obviously, 'Mopes' doesn't run that mansion for himself. It must be the mastermind himself who owns it, and he's the one we've got to get.'

'You really believe,' Ensdale asked, 'that a precipitate arrest of McCall would scare all the others away?'

'I'm darned, sure it would; that's why I'm having Gwenda trying to pump

McCall before we drop on him at his hideout.'

'In that case,' Ensdale said, 'there's nothing for it but for her to carry on — accept his invitation to go to the mansion with him. She might succeed on his 'home ground', as he calls it, and you'll have to arrange to stand by and see she isn't in too much danger.'

Dawson nodded slowly. 'Yes, I think that's it. She could also explore the place while she's there and see if she can spot anything suggestive of counterfeiting.'

'I could arrange it so that a wafer microphone is used there,' Harriday said. 'It will slip under a door or a French window somewhere, and give the boys a chance to record in a mobile unit. I could also watch that Gwenda is safe.'

'Uh-huh,' Dawson acknowledged. 'That's a good notion. I'd stay on tap in case we discover where the others in the gang can be located, then I can tip off the necessary men to get busy.'

'It also occurs to me,' Ensdale said, musing, 'that I may be able to help matters in general and this young woman in particular. I'll make up a phial of iltumine-X. If she can get a chance to drop some of it into his drink, he'll talk his head off. As you know, we've used it now and again to make stubborn ones open up a bit.'

'Illegal — but useful,' Dawson acknowledged, 'Okay, sir. That ought to be a grand help. Now I'd better give Gwenda the rough outline, then she'll know what to tell this gorilla when he rings her in the morning.'

In half an hour, Gwenda knew the particulars, and also that she must call in at the Yard the following day for a final check-up and to collect the phial which Ensdale would have ready for her. She knew exactly how tough her assignment was likely to be but, nevertheless, she did not flinch from it.

And, early the following morning, 'Mopes' phoned as he had promised, reversing the charge, as before.

'I've been thinking it over,' Gwenda responded, as his voice came through. 'I probably need my head examining, but I've decided to come along to your place this evening. How do I get there?'

'You don't, sweetheart! I pick you up in the car and take you there. An' you'll have ter forgive me if I just blindfold you.'

'What?'

'See the thing my way,' 'Mopes' insisted. 'You know what kind of a spot I'm in. I can't trust anybody — not even you — to see where I'm stayin'. If you agree to that, everythin' will be all right.'

'Very well,' Gwenda responded at last. 'Where will you meet me? Here?'

'No. That might be kinda risky. Y'know the Royal Garage, a few yards from your place?'

'On the corner? Yes — I know it.'

'Seven tonight, outside there. An', say . . .'

'Yes?'

'Wear that red dress you had on last night. I'm still thinkin' about it.'

'I'll do that,' Gwenda promised, making a grimace to herself. 'Seven tonight.'

The appointment made, she wasted no time in getting to the Yard to receive the final instructions. She found Chief-Inspector Dawson serious-faced but determined.

'Nobody could be more aware than I

am of the risk you are taking, Gwenda,' he said quietly. 'And we appreciate it. However, Sergeant Harriday here will keep an eye constantly to your welfare.'

Harriday beamed upon the girl as she glanced at him. 'Be a real pleasure, Miss Blane,' he promised.

'Whereabouts will you be?' she questioned.

For answer, Dawson spread out a sketch on the desk. The girl hunched forward in her chair and studied the diagram interestedly.

'This is a sketch of the mansion, as well as our boys could make it out in the moonlight last night, when they followed 'Mopes' back,' Dawson explained. 'Judging from the light in the curtained window on the ground floor here, this is the room 'Mopes' principally uses — and probably the one he will use tonight. Fortunately for us, it has a French window looking out on to the wooded grounds. Harriday here will be outside that window. Beneath its frame he'll push what we call a wafer microphone — a flat, disc-like affair, which will pick up every

151

sound from the room and transmit it to a mobile recording unit out in the side road here.' Dawson's finger stubbed the diagram. 'To the receiving unit, there'll be a subsidiary line wired back to a pair of headphones. Harriday will be wearing them and will therefore hear everything that is going on beyond the window. Clear so far?'

'Excellent!' Gwenda smiled. 'With so much reassurance, I'll give the vamp performance of my life!'

'If you find yourself getting into a difficult position with 'Mopes', just shout 'Help me quickly!' Harriday will take that as his signal to plunge in and rescue you. We hope that won't be necessary, because it'll spoil everything, but it's a wise precaution. Now — any questions you'd like to ask?'

'No, I don't think so. Assuming everything goes off all right, and I make 'Mopes' tell everything that's needful, do I walk out at the finish and leave him to it?'

'If you get everything needful from him, Harriday will step in at the finish in any case and arrest 'Mopes' on the spot. There will, of course, be several men about the grounds, ready for action. Summing it up,' Dawson finished, 'this is your great moment, Gwenda. And here is a phial of stuff which Mr. Ensdale has made up.'

'Oh, yes; you mentioned it. If I slip it into 'Mopes' drink, it'll make him talkative?'

'It should do, yes. Try it, anyhow.'

Gwenda slipped the phial into her handbag and then got to her feet.

'Well . . . here I go, Inspector. And I'll see you later on. You won't be at the mansion, I gather?'

'No. I'm staying here, so I can have all the necessary contacts in the event of urgent action being necessary. Good luck, Gwenda!'

She departed thoughtfully and spent the rest of the day in town, chiefly visiting a hair-stylist and a beauty parlour. Returning to her borrowed flat in mid-afternoon, she took her time over dressing in the cherry evening gown; then, when at last it was seven o'clock, she was outside the Royal Garage, hoping she would not get too disarranged in waiting for 'Mopes' to show up. The thought had barely passed through her mind before he drew up at the curb. Gwenda frowned a little as she beheld the expensive car. Evidently, 'Mopes' had somebody extremely influential behind him.

'That's my baby!' he exclaimed, alighting to the pavement and adjusting his tinted glasses. 'Hop in — front seat ... no, back seat,' he corrected. 'I'd forgotten the blindfold.'

'Do I have to do that?' Gwenda objected, settling down in the soft upholstery. 'Surely you don't think I'd give you away? I'd only make myself an accessory or something if I did. Hobnobbing with an escaped convict is an offence, remember.'

'I s'pose it is,' 'Mopes' agreed, reflecting: then his pig-eyes swept over the girl's exquisitely gowned form and up to her pretty, though still protesting, face.

'Please!' she said plaintively.

'Okay — forget it. As you said, if y'talk,

it'll only get you in bad, too. I'll risk it.'

With that, he slid back into the driving seat and set the car in motion again. Gwenda sank back into the cushions and tried to get control over her fast-beating heart. At the moment, in spite of the reassurances she had received from Dawson as to her welfare, she was feeling scared to death. The die was really cast and, as far as she could see, 'Mopes' could have only one object in view in taking her to the mansion where they could be alone. Then she felt around inside the voluminous folds of her skirt until she detected the hard outline of her loaded .32 automatic. That might save her if things got out of hand.

Once the main London traffic was left behind, she had not the vaguest idea where they were going. 'Mopes' hurtled the powerful car down dark lanes and twisting side streets, quite unaware, in his excitement and hurry, that he was being shadowed every inch of the way — not by a car, which would have given itself away by headlamps, but by a helicopter three hundred feet up, which was tracing him by the beams of his own headlights. Dawson had not left anything to chance. The mobile recording unit was already quite close to the mansion, but well concealed, and the various watchers had taken up their positions.

So, at length, 'Mopes' came to the end of the journey. With an unaccustomed gallantry, he helped the girl out of the car and then opened the mansion's front door. Still feeling oddly sick, she kept beside him as he went across the dark hall and presently switched on the lights of the drawing room.

'There!' he exclaimed proudly. 'Could you wish for anythin' better? I've spent all day dollin' it up.'

He pulled off his overcoat and hat and threw them on one side: then, tugging off his tinted glasses, he crossed to the coal fire and stirred it into a blaze. Meanwhile, the girl looked about her. Everything was certainly very comfortable and spacious. The French windows, she noticed, were masked by heavy purple drapes. She felt her breath catch a little as she detected, hardly visible, a flat disc, just discernible under the drapes. Evidently, it was Harriday's microphone, and unlikely to be seen unless deliberately looked for.

'Okay — let's have your cape,' 'Mopes' said, and whipped it from Gwenda's bare shoulders almost before she realized it. He laid it across a chair back and then went to the cocktail cabinet. Gwenda wandered to the chesterfield, still retaining her handbag. From it she surreptitiously took the phial of drug and kept it in her palm.

'Like the set-up?' 'Mopes' asked, coming back and sitting beside her as he handed a filled glass over. 'Cosy, huh?'

'Lovely,' Gwenda agreed. 'You've been working hard, Mr. McCall, to get it like this.'

'Worth it, ain't it? And call me 'Mopes'. Everybody else does. I don't like that 'mister' business.'

Gwenda smiled and raised her glass, then it suddenly slipped from her fingers and dropped on the floor, spilling its contents on the carpet.

'Well, of all the clumsy things!' She looked apologetic. 'I must be nervous. It dropped right out of my hand.'

'Think nothing of it, baby!'

'Mopes' got to his feet, balanced his drink on the arm of the chesterfield, then picked up the fallen glass after mopping the floor with his handkerchief. In the few moments he was at the cocktail cabinet filling another glass, Gwenda quickly rid herself of the phial's contents into his own glass.

'There!' he said, returning. 'Try again. And there ain't no need for you to be nervous. I ain't goin' to do anythin' to you. All I want is a woman to talk to, one who'll be friendly-like.'

'Oh — I see.' Gwenda drank slowly, watching him out of the corner of her eye.

'Y'know,' 'Mopes' went on, musing and drinking in turns, 'I've taken as big a risk as you in spendin' the evenin' like this. If the Chief wus to walk in and find us, he'd probably kill the pair of us. I'm not s'posed to have anybody here, 'less they're one of us. Too risky.'

Gwenda looked startled. 'Kill the pair of us? The sooner I get out, the . . . '

'Take it easy!' 'Mopes' caught her arm

as she half rose and pulled her back on to the chesterfield. 'It's a million t'one against him comin' in an', if he does, there will be a good warnin'. I spent quite a bit o' time riggin' a bell so that it'll ring if the front door opens. In that time, you can dodge behind them window drapes or some place.'

'Then you'd better put my cape out of sight. That'll be a complete give-away.'

'That's a thought,' 'Mopes' agreed. He finished his drink, got up, and then hid the cape by the simple expedient of putting it unceremoniously in one of the sideboard cupboards.

'Another drink?' he asked, pausing by the cabinet.

'Not right now.' Gwenda was feeling a trifle hazy even on one of the cocktails. 'Let's talk.'

'Fair enough.' 'Mopes' returned to her, frowning a little to himself. He could not quite understand why his heart was racing so violently. It wasn't fear, or emotion — not even indigestion. It was something he couldn't explain.

'Anything the matter?' Gwenda asked,

noticing he was anything but at ease.

'Nope. Just feel a bit tightened up, somehow. Mebbe your beauty's intoxicating me,' 'Mopes' added, with a grin.

Gwenda relaxed into the chesterfield's cushions. 'I say, 'Mopes' — who is his Chief of yours? He must be a clever man.'

'He's clever enough, but he's a dirty swine. No respect for other people's feelings. As for murder — he takes it in his stride.'

'Who is he really? I mean, do you know him?'

'Know him — ? 'Course I know him!'

'When I say that, I mean do you know who he really is? This crime racket is only a side line, surely?'

'You bet,' 'Mopes' acknowledged. 'An' don't let's waste time on 'im, baby. We've better things to do.'

'No harm in my asking questions, is there?'

'Nope — providing you don't ask too many.'

Gwenda tightened her mouth a little. She was still having the utmost difficulty in getting any information, and far from the mystery drug having made 'Mopes' talkative, it seemed, instead, to have made him rather impatient.

'Time's gettin' on,' he said presently. 'Don't you think we ought to know each other better?'

'In — what way?' Gwenda's blue eyes searched his ugly face.

For answer, he lunged suddenly forward towards her, his right arm encircling his waist and his left her shoulders. She was quite incapable of defending herself from the fierce, animal-like kisses he planted on her face and lips.

'That's better,' he grinned, straightening up again. 'Now we've made a start . . . '

Gwenda straightened up a little, breathing hard and trying not to show her real feelings. 'Mopes' studied her intently, his pig-eyes moving down from her face to her feet. Gwenda needed no imagination to guess what was in his mind.

'How — how many are there of you in this mansion in the ordinary way?' she asked, striving to keep her voice steady.

'Who cares?' 'Mopes' swung suddenly

to his feet, his face flushed. 'Get off that chesterfield, baby. I want to show you something.'

Gwenda hesitated and, at that, he grabbed her arm so savagely she gasped a little, his coarse nails cutting into her bare flesh. In one heave he had yanked her up.

'Know somethin'?' he muttered, holding her tightly against him. 'I think you've got other reasons for comin' here tonight than to just be with me. I've thought so all along, an' for that reason, I'm goin' to show you what it means to monkey around with 'Mopes' McCall!'

'You're crazy,' Gwenda said, as calmly as she could, and pulled herself free. 'My only reason for coming here is to be with you and, up to now, you've been a terrific flop. Unless you call that kissing act a good overture?'

She lounged away from him and he stood watching her, his eyes on the swing of her hips, the graceful curve of her back and shoulders. Then, suddenly, he muttered something unintelligible and lunged across the room.

Gwenda heard him coming and spun

round, her hand feeling instinctively for the gun in her skirt. Before she could get at it, he was upon her, his right hand seizing the front of her dress and wrenching it down the centre.

'That's better!' he grinned, as she recoiled and made vain efforts to cover herself up. 'Since you are an artist's model, you might as well pose for me. An' what in hell were you grabbin' at just now, when I came over here?'

He dived his hand at the skirt, ripping it savagely. The automatic fell out under such treatment and hit the carpet. Gwenda instantly dived for it, regardless of her efforts to hold her torn gown together, but one shove from 'Mopes' sent her stumbling away and he quickly snatched the gun up into his hand.

'Very pretty,' he sneered, glaring. 'So you come to spend the evening with me, an' pack a gun, huh?'

He stood thinking for a moment whilst Gwenda regarded him anxiously, her ruined dress hanging in tatters about her. Then he suddenly seemed to make up his mind. He threw the gun on the nearby table and came straight for her again. What happened in the ensuing moments, she had little idea. She was pushed and shoved and manoeuvred around until she, too, finally hit the chesterfield and sprawled upon it.

'This,' 'Mopes' panted, towering over her, 'is where we start to get real matey, sweetheart . . . '

He whipped off his jacket and grinned sadistically as she twisted her head to look at him. For the life of her, she could not remember the words of the emergency call she ought to give. Then 'Mopes' great body plunged down towards her, smashing the breath out of her.

It was at this identical moment that there came the crash of broken glass. 'Mopes' jerked up again, swearing, just in time to see a tall, broad-shouldered figure leaping across the room from the direction of the French windows.

'Who in hell . . . ?' 'Mopes' dragged to his feet, then he gasped as iron knuckles hit him under the chin and knocked him spinning against the table.

'Okay,' Harriday panted, as Gwenda

looked at him. 'I think I can handle this gentleman. I . . . '

'You'll handle nothin'!' 'Mopes' roared, as he realized Gwenda's automatic was right beside him on the table. 'I'll blow the livin' day . . . '

Harriday dived straight forward, in a rugby tackle. Since he did not have a gun, he had no alternative but his physique and agility. His arm locked around 'Mopes' legs and brought him down just as the gun went off. Then the fun really started.

Gwenda raised herself up to watch as the two men rolled furiously about the floor, battering and hammering at each other. First one took punishment and then the other. They got up, and smashed each other down again; and, out in the grounds, the various men posted at different positions were unaware that anything was wrong. They could not see the French windows from their vantage points, otherwise they would have noticed the gleam of light when Harriday had broken in. Nor were they near enough to hear the breaking of the glass, and in any case, the various shrubs around the house baffled the sound waves. As for the shot 'Mopes' had fired; the drapes had fallen back across the window and muffled it completely as far as outside hearing was concerned. Nothing could be heard at that distance.

Slowly, Harriday struggled to his feet, using the table to help him — and immediately 'Mopes' was up, too. He lashed out a jaw-breaking left, missed, and received one on the nose that drew blood. He swore, lunged, slamming a straight right into Harriday's stomach.

He was in anguish as the wind was blasted out of him. He bent double — to jerk straight again from a blinding uppercut that toppled him backwards. Senseless, he hit the carpet and sprawled.

The instant she saw what had happened, Gwenda lunged from the chesterfield and dived for the window, but 'Mopes' snatched her arm as she fled by. With a powerful twist, he swung her round, an unlovely vision, with blood smearing his face and his hair dishevelled.

'Nice work, baby,' he murmured,

tightening his hold. 'So you had your boy friend planted, did you? You damned cheap little bitch! I'll make you smart for this night's work, believe you me! I've a way of dealin' with women who try and double-cross me . . . '

He paused, staring at the floor near the door. Still retaining his steel grip on Gwenda's arm, he stooped and picked up the disc microphone. Its wire was still intact, though twisted. 'Mopes' pondered for several seconds until the truth crystallized in his slow-moving brain.

'So that's it!' He flung the mike down and drove his heel into it. 'Bin recordin' everything, huh? Cops just around the corner, and that mug was one of 'em in plain clothes. So you're workin' for the police? I was thinking as much! Right! Get movin' — an' quick!'

'Where — where to?' Gwenda was shaking, her eyes wild. She could not understand why no further help had arrived.

'I'll show you!' For answer 'Mopes' suddenly swung her over his massive shoulder, carried her from the room and up the staircase. She was aware of the cavernous darkness, of the corridor, and then light clicked on again and she found herself thrown down heavily upon a bed.

'Handy things, beds,' 'Mopes' said, with a brutal grin. 'I can tie you down and make you do as I say. Put a stop to your blasted struggling while I . . . '

'What's the idea, 'Mopes'?' a voice cut in.

'Mopes' swung round, bleary-eyed, and stared at the Chief as he stood in the doorway, a revolver in his hand.

'Hello, boss.' 'Mopes' straightened. 'I wus just going . . . '

'Shut up! Remember me saying some time ago I'd catch up with you one day? I seem to have done it. You're no longer any use to me. You've gummed up every damned thing from start to finish, bringing this girl here.'

'But listen, Chief, I . . . '

The Chief fired, and 'Mopes' didn't stand an earthly. The black hole from the bullet appeared on his gray shirt over his heart and he reeled heavily to the floor. Gwenda turned and looked at the quietly dressed man in the doorway. He came forward slowly, revolver still levelled.

'It's a pity you know so much, young woman,' he said, eyeing her disheveled hair and clothes. 'You've only yourself to thank, for mixing up with scum like 'Mopes' McCall. Sorry though I am, I have to dispose of you.'

Gwenda could only stare, too exhausted with reaction and fear to think of anything to say. Then, almost before she realized it, the Chief had snatched down one of the long curtain cords and began swiftly to bind her hands behind her. She made a brief, ineffectual struggle to get free, but had to give it up. Twisted on the bed, breathing hard, she found the Chief looking down at her.

'Apparently,' he said, 'Chief-Inspector Dawson has been surprisingly thorough. I noticed a mobile recording unit and men planted about the grounds as I arrived. In fact, the men in the recording van were wondering why recording had gone dead and were about to investigate. I managed to keep them away — as well as the men around the grounds. At the moment they have gone racing on a fool's errand, looking for 'Mopes' and you, and Detective Sergeant Harriday, whom I noticed lying flat out in the drawing room.'

'You — you sent the police away?' Gwenda stared incredulously. 'How could you? The head of this whole rotten outfit! How could you?'

'I have a way with me,' the Chief answered dryly. 'However, I am wasting time. Pardon me a moment.'

Turning aside, he removed his hat and coat. Gwenda lay helpless, trying to fathom why he was wearing a white coat. He looked like a house decorator, a soda-fountain operator — even a waiter. He was good looking after a fashion, unless it was a small graying imperial that conveyed the effect. In build, he was slight, but probably pretty strong. Then he turned and headed from the room.

That he had plenty of strength was revealed to her a few moments later, for he returned carrying Harriday's unconscious form in a fireman's lift. He dumped him near the bed, against the wall, and swiftly went to work to bind him up with the remaining curtain cord.

'Everything neat and tidy . . . ' The Chief made a final examination of Gwenda's painfully tight cords, looked at the sprawled body of 'Mopes', with the burn-hole over his heart, then he carefully re-donned his hat and coat. Evidently he had only removed them during his exertions so as to have more freedom.

'This place contains so much of interest to the police if they return here, as they inevitably will, that I have decided to burn it down,' he explained. 'Fire is such a wonderful element, don't you think?'

He smiled slowly, his rapier-like cold grey eyes on the girl's face; then he turned aside and removed something from his pocket. It looked purplish as it lay in his hand after being shaken out of a small envelope.

'Permanganate of potash,' he explained, seeing her eyes fixed upon him. 'I pour them on the carpet, so, and . . . '

They streamed from his hand into a

little pyramid. Then he held up a bottle of transparent bluish substance.

'Glycerine,' he concluded. 'Just an old chemical trick to produce a delayed action fire, you see. I pour the glycerine on the permanganate, and you notice it froths up. In a few minutes, during which time I'll have time to get clear, it will smoke and burst into flame.'

He straightened up and turned away quickly. 'Sorry I cannot stay longer. Goodbye!'

The door slammed and Gwenda lay staring like one hypnotized as — true to prediction — the crystals presently began to smoke, to glow, and then they burst into flame and filled the air with the stench of burning carpet.

7

It took several seconds for Gwenda to realize that this was the end — that, in a very short time, the place would be in flames. Immediately she realized it, she began rolling herself desperately on the bed, finally dropping herself with painful impact to the floor. Twisting again, she seized one of the fallen blankets in her teeth and attempted to drag it along towards the now smouldering fire in the carpet and smother it; but long before her attempt could succeed, the smouldering became flame, and she had to roll in the opposite direction to save herself.

The window! Was that a possibility? No use if there were no men in the grounds any more, and she couldn't get free of her ropes, no matter how hard she tried. She coughed as smoke surged into her lungs and gave a desperate look around her. Then, to her amazement, she saw something quite unbelievable. 'Mopes'

McCall, despite the obvious bullet wound over his heart, was slowly sitting up and rubbing his head dazedly.

' 'Mopes'!' Gwenda's voice was a scream. ' 'Mopes' — you're not dead!'

'Huh?' He shook himself and looked about him, then he gave a start as he saw the smouldering fire.

'What the hell . . . ?'

'The Chief did it!' Gwenda chattered on. 'Tied me up, along with the Sergeant there, and set the place on fire with glycerine or something. He didn't bother to tie you up since I suppose he thought you were dead. Get us free — quick!'

'Mopes' heaved to his feet, feeling at himself and frowning. Then, from his shirt pocket, over the heart, he drew forth his thick notebook and examined it. In a dazed fashion he peered at a bullet embedded within it.

'Can you beat that?' he asked. 'The slug lost itself in me notebook — an' the Chief didn't kill me, as he intended to. Ain't that nice? Ain't that really nice?' His face hardened brutally as he threw the book away.

' 'Mopes' — for the love of heaven . . .' Gwenda coughed savagely. 'Get us out of here — the Sergeant and me. I'll do whatever you want afterwards. Get us clear of this fire.'

'Mopes' looked at it, seeing it was now beyond all control.

'I've no time,' he said curtly. 'I've a score to settle with the Chief. Will his face be red when I turn up to settle with him!'

He hurtled for the door and Gwenda's despairing voice came to him again:

' 'Mopes' — you can't do it! You can't leave me and the Sergeant here . . .'

'Who can't? What the hell did either of you do for me but get me into the hell of a mess?' Just the same, 'Mopes' still hesitated. Gwenda was a woman, and a highly desirable one at that. Perhaps if he . . . No! No use slipping back again. She and he were on opposite sides of the fence.

'I've a job to do!' he snapped. 'I'm going straight to the Chief's home and straighten things up with him.'

Then he was gone and the door slammed amidst a swirl of smoke. Out in the corridor, he found the air comparatively clear and he wasted no time in hurrying down into the basement laboratory. Here he collected the double blowpipe, a capsule of darts, and then went on his way, homicidal viciousness in every line of his ugly face.

Meantime, Gwenda had rolled herself away from the immediate source of the fire.

By degrees she reached the spot where Harriday was lying and dimly showing signs of returning consciousness after the shattering blow in the jaw he had taken. When at last Gwenda did reach him, she did the only thing she could do to arouse him — lay flat on her back and dug her feet into him repeatedly — a performance calling for considerable effort with her legs and arms bound as they were.

After a while he responded and opened his eyes. Since neither the Chief nor 'Mopes' had switched off the light, he was able immediately to take in the situation — and what he saw and smelled dashed the last fogs of unconsciousness from his mind.

'We've got to do something — and quickly,' Gwenda told him, raising her head and shoulders to look at him. 'It won't be long before that burning carpet sets fire to the furniture and the bedding; then we'll really be in a mess.'

'Can't understand where the boys are, that they don't come,' Harriday muttered, straining savagely at the cord tethering him. 'They must have an idea how things are . . . '

'The Chief sent them away. He told me that when he set the place on fire.'

Harriday stopped struggling. 'The Chief did? What in hell's the matter with our fellows to take orders from him?'

'I don't know — and, right at this moment, I don't care. What do we do? We've got to move fast . . . oh, 'Mopes' has gone! I thought he'd been shot dead, but he wasn't. The bullet stuck in his notebook. He's gone to square accounts with the Chief.'

Harriday muttered something at the turn events had taken, and then looked about him.

'Main thing is to get rid of these ropes,'

he said. 'I can't get at the knife in my pocket, and I don't think you could, either. Nor will it be safe to try and wriggle over the burning carpet there and let it burn the ropes through: too painful and too likely to set our clothes on fire. So what the devil do . . . I have it!' he exclaimed abruptly. 'You say 'Mopes' just left here?'

'Uh-huh.' Gwenda waited anxiously.

'Did he lock the door there?'

'Not as far as I know. He just slammed it.'

'Good! Then it's worth the effort of rolling to it and trying to get into the corridor outside. What I'm thinking of is the bathroom. There ought to be a razor there, since 'Mopes' is clean shaven. Or else a razor blade. We'll be free in no time if that's the case . . . let's go!'

Without delaying any longer, they began dragging and rolling themselves towards the door, avoiding the burning area and coughing with every movement they made — so thick had the smoke become.

'So far, so good!' Harriday panted, as

they gained the door. 'Now for the tough part. Maybe I can brace myself.'

He rolled and manoeuvred until his shoulders were against the door itself. Then, digging his heels into the carpet, he levered himself up inch by inch, using the door to support his back. Thuswise, he finally became upright enough to have the doorknob on a line with his bound hands. Gripping it with difficulty with his finger ends, he turned the knob and then toppled forward, dragging the door open with him.

The rest was again a matter of manoeuvre and wriggling as they both eased themselves out into the corridor. Having succeeded so far, and having clear air again to breath, they were encouraged in their efforts. Certainly they had no idea where the bathroom was, but it had got to be found.

'Stay here if you wish, whilst I look,' Harriday said, peering at the girl in the faintly reflected moonlight through the corridor window.

'Not on your life! I'm rolling as far from that burning bedroom as possible!'

So the painful, laborious progress was resumed — and for quite a while it was without result. They opened quite a few doors with considerable difficulty, to find they gave on to empty rooms — but at last they found the one they sought, and Harriday wasted no time in edging himself in a series of long, kangaroo-like leaps towards the mirrored cupboard over the washbowl.

He turned the cupboard catch back with his teeth and then looked into the interior. His eyes gleamed at the sight of a number of old razor blades carelessly flung into a grimy looking tumbler. Again his teeth came into action and he lifted the tumbler out and then deliberately dropped it.

It splintered on the uncarpeted flooring beside the bowl, scattering glass and old razor blades all over the floor.

'That's it!' Gwenda cried in delight.

'Yes — but keep clear, or those bare arms of yours might get badly cut. I'm okay in this jacket — I hope! Here I go!'

He flattened himself down carefully and spent the next five minutes working into a position where his carefully investigating fingers could pick up either a blade or a piece of glass. It happened to be a blade and, after that, the rest was easy. Three or four edgewise movements with the blade cut the rope on his wrists and he quickly pulled himself free. In one minute flat he also had Gwenda free and helped her to her feet. She was looking about her in the dim light, doing what she could to fasten her rent garments in place.

'Here, take this,' Harriday said, tugging off his coat. 'Make you feel less embarrassed, maybe. And much warmer.'

'Thanks.' She took it gratefully and buttoned it about her. 'I've got a cape in the drawing room, but maybe this is no time to think about it.'

'Grab it as we go out,' Harriday said, diving for the door. 'You've put up with enough without losing a cape as well. Come on.'

She kept beside him as they hurried down the staircase. By this time, flames were crackling from the bedroom they had vacated, and the whole big house was full of smoke. Gwenda detoured long enough to recover her cape from the sideboard cupboard, and then hurried with Harriday to the outdoors — just as a party of men came running up. From the distance there came the sound of a fire engine's siren.

'Thompson!' Harriday exclaimed, halting as the men came up. 'Where in blazes have you men been all this time? Didn't you know Miss Blane and I were in real trouble?'

'We thought you might be, Sergeant, when the microphone blanked out but, just at that moment, Mr. Ensdale came along with the news that you and Miss Blane had been spirited away round the back by 'Mopes'. He told us which way you'd gone, so we followed hell for leather. When we couldn't find any trace of you, we came back to make sure. I sent one of the boys to phone the fire brigade when we spotted smoke coming from an upper window.'

'Who did you say came along?' Harriday asked, in wonderment.

'Mr. Ensdale. I assumed he was

deputizing for the Inspector while he remained at the Yard . . . '

'And when he'd given you these instructions, what did he do?'

Thompson scratched the back of his head. 'Don't rightly know, sir. We left him here.'

'Oh, you did . . . ' Harriday thought swiftly, then:

'Have your men do what they can to examine this house before it all caves in. There must be traces of the counterfeiting apparatus somewhere. Then get us to your car, and give me your phone.'

'Right!' Thompson turned and gave his orders. By the time he had done so, the fire engine was sweeping up the driveway.

'Look after them, Mason,' Thompson ordered, and then quickly led the way to the nearby squad car. Harriday and Gwenda tumbled into the back whilst Thompson took up his position beside the driver.

As they moved off, Harriday wasted no time in getting through to Whitehall — and Dawson. In silence the Chief-Inspector listened to the story Harriday had to tell.

'I just can't understand it,' Harriday finished in perplexity. 'I can concede that you appointed Ensdale to supervise things here for you, but I can't fathom why he gave an order which led all our men off trail, and nearly cost Gwenda and me our lives.'

'Time you tumbled to the truth, Bob — as I did some time ago,' Dawson replied briefly. 'I never gave Ensdale any sanction to act on my behalf. I've quite sufficient faith in you. What you have told me simply confirms what I have suspected for a long time. Namely, that Ensdale and the Chief of the counterfeit racket are one and the same person.'

'What? That's stretching things too far, sir . . . '

'Not at all. Why did Ensdale persistently claim that all the snakebites were genuine? Why did Maudie Vincent die so suddenly after Ensdale had called to see her — and probably slipped her something that finished her? Why did he insist on being present at our final conference to see how things were going, as he put it?

Lastly, he's one of the cleverest physicists we've got. There's a host of reasons why it must be he, Bob, and I rather expected he'd betray himself tonight, which is one reason why I kept out of the picture. Anyhow, I can't explain more now. I'm acting immediately to have him arrested. He'll probably be at his home, satisfied that he has rid himself of all danger. See you later.'

With that, Dawson ended the call, and Harriday looked at Gwenda.

'Well?' she asked quickly, as she settled herself beside him. 'What did the Inspector say?'

'Plenty — but the main thing is that he's going after Ensdale. He's the man we've been looking for all this time!'

'Mr. Ensdale?' Thompson repeated, turning sharply in his seat. 'But surely that's wrong? He's . . . '

'Dawson's satisfied, Thompson, so there's nothing I can say. Look, Gwenda; have you ever seen Mr. Ensdale yourself?'

'No.'

'Then — what did the Chief look like when he burst in upon you tonight?'

'Oh — middle-aged. Hair going a bit grey. Spare build. Very piercing grey eyes. Quiet way of talking, but very purposeful. Oh, yes — he had a little imperial.'

Harriday smiled wryly. 'Ensdale to the life — except for the beard. Presumably he wears that as a slight disguise. I assume he had no beard when he spoke to you and the boys, Thompson?'

'No, sir.'

'No wonder he knew so much,' Harriday mused. 'However, maybe we'll learn more at the Yard. Carry on, Thompson, and let's see what's happened. I have the feeling that maybe 'Mopes' McCall will settle everything for us. He'll be the last person Ensdale will expect to see.'

'And 'Mopes' won't even have to search for him,' Gwenda put in. 'You probably heard him say, over the mike, that he knows the Chief's real identity?'

Harriday nodded and relapsed into moody silence as the car got under way again — and, at about this time, another car, driven by 'Mopes', the one he usually used, was drawing up at the corner of

Endersby Place in Central London. Some distance along Endersby Place was the Georgian-style home of Boyd Ensdale, as the ex-convict very well knew.

Alighting from the car, 'Mopes' locked it and then moved with purposeful strides down the street, pausing when he came opposite to number seventeen. It lay on the opposite side of the street so, well out of range of the nearest street lamp, 'Mopes' pondered the house carefully. It was solid, as became its period, and was one of a row.

There was light behind the curtains of the downstairs room and the front door came flush with the street.

'Mopes' eyes rose to the upper rooms. No lights came from there, but there was a network of solidly built drainpipes, with the main drainpipe connected between numbers seventeen and nineteen.

'Easy,' he muttered, ''specially at this time of night.'

He glanced once more up and down the street, noted that it was deserted, and then sped swiftly across it. Shinning up a drainpipe, especially such an easy one, was no task to 'Mopes' and, in thirty seconds, he had reached the bedroom window. The old-fashioned catch responded instantly to his penknife and, hardly making a sound, he slid into the room and closed the window softly.

His training as a housebreaker led him to keep quiet for several seconds, 'smelling' things out, as he called it, and accustoming his eyes to the gloom. By degrees, he made out the room's detail in the reflected glow from the lamp further down the street. There was the bed, the usual furniture — and that was that.

'No antidote likely to be 'ere,' he told himself. 'On your way, feller!'

He drifted to the door, opened it, and peered out into the passageway. Everything quiet and dark. He passed along it, crept down the stairs, and finally paused at the door under which there lay a bar of light — the room he had seen from the street. Listening outside it, he heard the rustle of paper now and again, and a slight cough.

Finally, he looked through the keyhole, and could see part of an armchair, a glowing fire, and the lower half of a man's profile. There was no doubt that it was Boyd Ensdale, minus his torpedo beard, and also minus the white surgical coat that he had been wearing earlier.

'So you sit there and read, calm as you like, after tryin' to kill me, huh?' 'Mopes' whispered, straightening again. 'You're in for one helluva shock, believe me!'

Satisfied that his victim was alone and just 'asking for it', 'Mopes' prowled again until he came to the door that led to the cellar, a region inseparable from the house architecture. Below there might be that which he sought.

He crept down into the darkness, taking care to shut the upper door behind him. For light he used what few matches he had with him and presently discovered he was in a cellar that had been converted into a scientific laboratory.

'Just as I'd 'oped,' 'Mopes' murmured and, using up his precious matches, he began a search of the shelves, peering at the neatly labelled bottles. He was commencing to fear he would never find that which he was seeking when a bottle apart from the others, quarter full of a transparent liquid, caught his eye. The label said: 'Anti-Ser-Rat', which, to 'Mopes' ponderous brain finally suggested 'Antidote-Serum-Rattlesnake', or something like it.

'Chance it, anyway,' he murmured and, taking the bottle from the shelf, he poured its contents down the sink and re-filled it with water. Replacing the bottle in the exact spot, he crept silently back up the stairs and re-opened the door into the hall.

To his horror, the full-bodied glare of a torch struck him in the eyes and, from behind it, came a faint gasp of surprise. Instinctively, he slammed the door shut again and flung himself down the steps as a gun exploded in the hall, whanging a bullet clean through the door panel.

'Mopes' reached the cellar floor and half fell over. He had a pretty good mental impression of his surroundings, and quickly fled to one of the far corners, behind the staircase. Here he worked rapidly in the darkness, bringing out his double blowpipe and loading it from the capsule. It was no easy job in the dark, but long practice with the fiendish darts had made him a past master.

Then the lights came on full blaze and there were cautious footsteps on the stone steps. 'Mopes' still waited and, at length, the voice of the Chief reached him:

'No use your skulking down there, 'Mopes'. From upstairs I can operate a switch that will fill this basement with chlorine gas and choke the life out of you. Before I do that, though, be kind enough to enlighten me as to how you come to be here. I fully believed I'd finished with you.'

'Mopes' did not answer. He was watching and listening keenly, his blow-pipe ready for action.

'A pity you won't explain it,' the Chief said in regret. 'I have to think I miscalculated. However, since you won't talk to me, I may as well talk to you — perhaps cheer you on your way to the Eternity to which you are certainly going. This evening, whilst engaged with the delectable Gwenda Blane, you probably found your emotions were out of hand, that you were even more bestial than usual. In case your dumb brain has been puzzled by that, I should explain that I prepared a special drug to create just that effect on your nerve-centres, and I'm sure the resourceful Miss Blane would find a means somehow to add the drug to your drink.'

'Mopes' eyes narrowed as he remembered the incident of the girl's fallen glass. Less clearly, he recalled his own queer feelings and the subhuman promptings that had assailed him.

'I flatter myself I calculated everything very nicely,' the Chief continued. 'I reasoned you would go berserk, that Sergeant Harriday would break in to the rescue of the lady, and that you probably would get yourself arrested. Things did not happen quite that way — but at least I achieved my main object, which was to have you so out of hand that you would not tell that girl anything. I hope you didn't become sentimental and save them from the fire which I started?'

'No, I . . . ' 'Mopes' checked himself, annoyed that he had broken his silence, but it was too late now. He heard the feet coming lower down the steps. He stood crouching and waited, blowpipe ready.

'Incidentally, 'Mopes',' the voice added, 'you ought to have more sense than enter the home of a scientist, and imagine you are safe. I have quite a few photo-electric cells scattered around to protect myself against intruders, an essential precaution to a man of my — er — unorthodox pursuits. Several times the warning light flashed in my drawing room, so there is no mystery about my knowing you were present — or at least, that somebody was . . .'

The voice stopped suddenly and, in an opposite corner of the basement, something clattered noisily. The gangster swung towards it, his heart pumping and, in a matter of seconds, he saw it was a golden cigarette case, which had been thrown to distract his attention. He grasped all this in split seconds, but in those split seconds lay a fatal gap. Boyd Ensdale jumped the remainder of the steps, swung his gun, and fired. Once — twice — three times.

'Mopes' twitched and gasped as the bullets bit into him. He fell on his face, the still loaded blowpipe in his hand underneath him. He could still think in a hazy kind of way, but his body would hardly respond. It was clamped in the steel vice of an ever-increasing pain.

'No mistake this time, my friend,' Ensdale said in cold tones. 'And floric acid can very soon take care of your complete elimination. I only wish I knew when Harriday and Gwenda Blane died — or if they did. They can make things somewhat difficult for me if they have the chance to speak to Thompson and his group of dolts . . . '

By this time, Ensdale was half talking to himself. He took a final look at the motionless 'Mopes' as he finished speaking, and then turned away towards a gutta-percha carboy which evidently contained the floric acid he had spoken of.

'Mopes' was subconsciously aware of the movements, of the scrape of feet on the floor, and it penetrated his dying brain that he had left his scheme of revenge unfinished — which gave him just the necessary urge to finish the job.

With a stupendous effort, he raised himself on one elbow and fixed Ensdale's back with malignant eyes. Shakily, he put the blowpipe to his lips and, with deliberation and literally his last breath, blew the darts. Then he was dead, the blowpipe clattering from his hand.

Ensdale turned, clutching the back of his neck as he felt the vicious sting of the poisoned icicles. He wrenched them out and stamped on them, stared at 'Mopes', then again brought out his gun and fired twice into the corpse. This done, he turned swiftly, took the snake-bite antidote from the shelf and filled a hypodermic syringe as quickly as possible.

The syringe loaded, he whipped off his jacket and rolled up his shirt-sleeve . . .

'Stand right where you are, Mr. Ensdale!'

He looked up with a start. So preoccupied had he been in his own physical danger, he had not thought of, nor heard, anything else. Now he beheld the grim-faced Chief-Inspector Dawson on the steps and, behind him, were three constables. But none of them appeared to be armed — a fact that made Ensdale smile rather bitterly. He hesitated for a second, deciding whether to use his gun or not; then his natural coolness came to his rescue.

'Well, gentlemen — I'm standing. What's the matter?' Dawson finished the journey from the steps and came across, as Ensdale slowly lowered his shirt-sleeve again.

'Not much use my wasting time, Ensdale,' Dawson said. 'You're under arrest. I'll complete the formalities at the station. Meantime, it's my duty to warn you . . . '

'Don't recite that rubbish to me, Dawson.' Ensdale adjusted his cuff-link. 'For what am I under arrest? What's the charge?'

'Murder, attempted murder, counterfeiting, and arson.' Dawson gave a dry smile. 'Practically everything in the book, I'd say.'

Ensdale leaned casually against the bench, trying not to show in his expression the pain he was commencing to experience as the snake venom bit through the bloodstream.

'You know, Dawson, I've always had quite a respect for your abilities, but I'm becoming discouraged. When you creep into my house and indict me as a common criminal, you're laying yourself open to plenty of trouble. I'm sure the Assistant Commissioner won't approve what I tell him.'

'You can stop bluffing,' Dawson said briefly; then, reaching forward suddenly, he removed the bulge from Ensdale's right-hand pocket and handed it to the constable behind him. Ensdale watched, and his eyes were straying to the dead 'Mopes' in the corner.

Dawson saw the movement and strolled over to the corpse. He examined it briefly; then, pulling on his gloves, he carefully took up the blowpipe and dropped it into the cellophane envelope that he withdrew from his pocket.

'Your very active snake, I assume?' he asked, coming back to where the scientist was half crouched by the bench, biting his underlip to keep control of himself.

'Stop — stop jumping to conclusions,' Ensdale said. 'You can never do anything to me, or anybody else without absolute proof — and that you haven't got! You can find a man over a corpse, the knife still gripped from the fatal blow: but if you haven't seen the fatal blow, and got witnesses to prove it, you're lost. Or do I need to remind you of that loophole in English law, known as 'the reasonable doubt'?'

'You always did know how to talk, Ensdale,' Dawson said curtly, 'but on this occasion I've no time to waste. Take him away, boys, and one of you phone for an anbulance to remove our lamented friend on the floor there . . .'

The constables began moving — and so did Ensdale. He turned abruptly and, from the shelf over the bench behind him, snatched down a phial of what appeared to be glycerine. With it upraised in his hand, he faced Dawson again.

'No you don't, Dawson!' he snapped. 'I'll not be ordered about by you, your confounded men, or anybody else! Lay a hand on me, and I'll drop this — and that will be the finish for the lot of us. It's mercury fulminate, in case you're wondering, and there's enough here to blow this house and its immediate neighbors to Hades.'

Dawson tightened his lips, signalling the constables to make no further move. For a moment or two there was silence, and Dawson was the first to break it.

'You know as well as I do that you can't keep this up indefinitely, Ensdale! Put that damned stuff down and behave with some sense!'

Ensdale winced as a spasm shot through him. His face went a sickly shade of grey.

'Stop giving me orders, Dawson! I'm the one who can afford to do that at the moment, and I'm telling you to get off my premises, and take your men with you. I'll give you half a minute, and if you don't, I'm going to drop this bottle. I'd prefer we all get blown to bits than that you should nail me.'

'Which is as good as admitting that my accusations against you are correct?'

Ensdale did not answer. He bent

slightly under the tightening anguish of the snake venom. Dawson moved forward slowly until he had reached the bench.

'What's the matter with you?' he demanded. 'You feeling ill?'

'Mind your own business!' Ensdale straightened up again, his upraised hand quivering dangerously.

'I'll make one guess,' Dawson said, abruptly snatching up something from the bench. 'You're hoping to use this!'

Ensdale breathed hard as he looked at the hypodermic, ready filled for use, in Dawson's hand.

'Give that to me,' he whispered. 'I'm going to drop this bottle if you don't!'

Dawson took a step or two back, shaking his head. 'I don't think you will, Ensdale. You love life as much as anybody else, and you'll not kill yourself as long as you can overcome that snakebite venom. That's obviously what's wrong with you. The blow-pipe on the floor beside 'Mopes'; you with your shirt-sleeve up as we came in; this hypo, ready filled . . . '

'Give — it — to — me!'

'I'll give it to you on two conditions.

200

One of them is that you give me that mercury fulminate, and the other is that you admit the facts I have already outlined. We can save a lot of time that way, and I have my witnesses right here.'

'That's damned unethical, Dawson — and you know it full well! No policeman can enforce a confession under duress.'

'Technically, no — but I'm entitled to use any means I consider advisable to get at the truth — and that's what I mean to do.'

Ensdale glowered, perspiration commencing to trickle down his face. Then, after a few seconds, he handed over the mercury fulminate, which Dawson promptly gave gingerly to the care of the officer nearest him.

'Well?' Dawson raised an eyebrow. 'You are the man we're looking for, aren't you?'

'Yes.' Ensdale did not make any attempt at denial this time. 'And I'd have got away with it, maybe for years, if that bonehead 'Mopes' hadn't gummed things up . . .'

'Your statements about the snakebites were necessarily false, because you wanted to safeguard yourself?'

'Naturally. You'd have done the same.'

'I'm not concerned with what I'd have done. I'm concerned with the fact that you never proved the presence of saliva, the one thing that would have proved the claim of genuine snakebite. I was also struck by the surprising coincidence of Maudie Vincent having a relapse after you called to see her at the hospital. Obviously, you fixed that relapse very neatly.'

Ensdale shrugged. 'Snake venom was already known to be in her system, though neutralized. The presence of a little more would not excite suspicion — nor did it. I merely gave her a second shot, so that she would not talk too much.'

'You are remarkably frank,' Dawson remarked, vaguely puzzled.

'Why not? Having admitted one thing, I might as well admit the remainder . . .' But, just the same, there was an enigmatic light in Ensdale's sharp eyes. He appeared to be thinking swiftly.

'I assume you insisted on joining our final conference so that you could discover exactly what we meant to do?'

'Naturally.'

'I'm glad you did. I'd suspected you for a long time, and that move satisfied me. You had no real need to be so interested, not being actively engaged on the case, beyond the pathological side. Very ingenious, Ensdale. An imperial beard for the Chief, and none for Ensdale. Right?'

Ensdale mopped his face. 'For God's sake, Dawson, stop playing around with me and hand over that hypo. I can't stand any more of this!'

Dawson complied and watched in silence as Ensdale quickly bared his arm again and sank the needle into a vein. He depressed the hypo-plunger to its limit and then smiled grimly to himself.

'That's better!' he said, in relief, 'or will be, when it gets circulating. Well, gentlemen — anything more?'

'We'll be moving,' Dawson said. 'And I'm glad to see you are taking this business sensibly, Ensdale.'

Ensdale drew on his jacket and buttoned it precisely.

'Before we go, Dawson, I have one or two experiments in progress in this basement. Have I your permission to switch off the current?'

'Go ahead,' Dawson agreed, watching narrowly. 'But don't try anything funny.'

The scientist turned away to a switch panel, pulled out a number of plugs, snapped over several make-and-break switches, and then looked about him.

'I'm ready,' he said, but in striding forward he bent double and nearly fell to his knees. Immediately, Dawson and one of the constables helped him to straighten again. There was anguish in every line of his face.

'The — the antidote's a long time working,' he panted slowly. 'I only hope you didn't let me have it too late, Dawson. If you did, that makes you a murderer, too.'

'Or an unwitting judge.' Dawson answered. 'We'll give you a hand up the steps.'

'No — no — I don't need that. I can

do it better by myself. You needn't think I'm trying to attempt anything. I'm far too ill for that.'

Holding his middle and biting at his lips to stifle cries of pain, Ensdale tottered to the steps and began to climb them. Dawson nodded to his men and began to follow. He kept immediately behind Ensdale until the top stair was reached, then the scientist unexpectedly swung round and lashed out his foot. How much the effort cost him in physical anguish could not be measured. All Dawson knew was that he received the savage blow straight in the face, the whole world seeming to explode in sparks around him. He stumbled backwards, knocking over the man coming behind him.

Then Ensdale was beyond the doorway to the hall, and it closed with a violent bang.

8

Dazed, blood streaming from his face from a deep gash in his cheek, Dawson struggled upright again as his men helped him.

'Never mind me!' he panted, whipping out his handkerchief. 'Get after Ensdale — quick!'

At that, one of the men bounded to the top of the stairs and shoved violently on the tightly locked door. In a moment or two he was reinforced by his colleagues and, in unison, they shoved and kicked against the panels, without result. Dawson watched them, mopping his face and fuming by turns.

'Get something from below,' he ordered. 'There must be a something we can use as a jemmy, or a crowbar or . . . ' He stopped, breaking off into a fit of uncontrollable coughing as a heavy odour wafted past him and nearly stopped his breathing.

'That's chlorine gas!' one of the men

exclaimed, startled. 'I'd know it anywhere.'

'Gas — gas — or otherwise, we want something to open this door!' Dawson got his voice back with an effort; then he turned to attempt the task himself, using his handkerchief both to cover his mouth and protect his gashed cheek.

It was when he reached the floor of the basement, the coughing men coming down behind him, that he realized how dense the gas was becoming. It could be heard hissing somewhere.

'Ensdale must have done this when he monkeyed around with that switchboard,' one of the men said, looking about him with watering eyes. 'If we could find where . . . there!' And he pointed to a nozzle projecting from a tank rather like an oxygen cylinder.

Even to approach it, however, was useless. It was emitting the deadly gas freely, and its nozzle was electrically controlled. To deal with it without masks was a hopeless proposition.

'Here!' Dawson had been exploring hastily, and now started to unclamp a heavy vice from the bench.

'This ought to smash the door through.'

Coughing and gasping, their eyes watering as the choking fumes grew denser around them, the men began to struggle with the clamps of the vice and, at last, got it free. It took two of them to carry it up the steps. Dawson and the remaining man followed them, handkerchiefs pressed to their faces.

In three massive blows, the vice crashed through the wood of the hall door — but, instead of tumbling into the hall beyond, it clanged against something metallic, and then fell down into a cavity beyond the door.

'I'll be damned!' Dawson muttered. 'A steel slide. We can't get through that. Evidently Ensdale had this house of his fixed for any eventuality.'

The four men looked at each other anxiously, struggling to get some fresh air into their lungs — then one of them snapped his fingers.

'This basement may originally have been a coal cellar! There could be a grid or something to throw the coal through!'

Immediately they blundered down the steps again, hurrying into the basement beyond the laboratory section. Here the air was a trifle clearer, but their hopes of a coal chute or grid were instantly dashed. A steel slide was in position here, too, fixed in well-greased grooves, and probably electrically controlled from somewhere in the house above. Every means of escape was sealed.

'Damned cunning swine, isn't he?' Dawson muttered, still mopping his damaged face. 'Only one thing for it, boys, if we don't want to be choked to death mighty soon.'

'What's that, sir? Try and smash a way through the wall?'

'No. That wouldn't do any good. I was thinking of that mercury fulminate. Which one of you has it?'

One of the men looked rather astonished, and then scared. Carefully, he felt in his uniform jacket and finally produced the phial. Dawson took it and gave a frown.

'To the best of my knowledge, mercury

fulminate is a form of greyish crystal,' he said. 'This is either mixed with something else to give it its syrupy look, or else Ensdale was just bluffing, knowing we wouldn't dare argue!'

In fascination, the constables watched as he uncorked the bottle and sniffed at it. He smiled bitterly.

'Acetone! Can't you smell the peppermint?'

'I can't smell anything but that damned chlorine!' one of the constables muttered, 'and it's getting thicker, sir. Ensdale was fooling, then?'

'Obviously. He knew we'd not dare to argue, and probably imagined that, since he is a physicist, we'd think he'd doctored the stuff up somehow. Fact remains it's no use . . . better see what else there is.'

They returned into the laboratory section of the basement, but they could only search for a few minutes before they found the fumes of the still escaping chlorine gas too much for them. They retreated into a far corner of cellar without having accomplished anything, and even here, the fumes were becoming denser, keeping all of them in a constant state of coughing.

'Surely,' one of the constables asked, 'there ought to be an acetylene cutter in a laboratory like this?'

'Very probably,' Dawson agreed, 'but when you're nearly knocked senseless by the gas, what's the use of trying to search? If any of you men have lungs strong enough to cap that chlorine nozzle, we might accomplish something; I can't do it — I'm bronchial even in the normal way.'

One of the constables suddenly made up his mind, driven by the desperate thought that death was the answer if something was not done immediately. He took as deep a breath as he dared of the mephitic atmosphere, then set off with his handkerchief clamped to his mouth and nose. The others watched him, struggling desperately to keep their senses.

After a while, however, the constable came back, and allowed his pent-up breath to escape in an explosive gasp.

'That — that's not doing the damage, sir!' he panted. 'It's empty and labelled 'oxygen'. There's a sealed oxygen cylinder above it, and another one of sealed hydrogen on top of that. The chlorine is at the very top, coming from a jet let into the wall. Can't do a thing about it . . . we got the wrong idea.'

'Oh — hell!' Dawson looked about him in desperation; then, quite suddenly, his eyes gleamed. 'Wait! Did you say a cylinder of oxygen and one of hydrogen? Sealed?'

'According to the labels on them — yes.'

'I've got to have them! Also that empty Dewar flask from by the wall there.'

The constable nodded, but Dawson did not expect him to do the task all by himself. He jerked his head and advanced, holding his breath as much as possible, disregarding the ooze of blood still trickling down his cheek.

To remove the two unwanted cylinders was not difficult, with four of them to handle the job and, in the process, they could see the jet from which the chlorine was apparently coming. It was too high up to be got at, however, let alone capped, and in any case, Dawson seemed to be in possession of some new idea.

Under his directions, as they battled with their tortured lungs, the cylinders were carried to the top of the stone steps, whilst Dawson and the remaining man brought the big Dewar flask, probably used originally for the storage of liquid air. Up at the summit of the steps, the chlorine gas was not so dense, due mainly to its fairly heavy specific gravity, which kept it, as yet, at the lower levels.

'What's the idea, sir?' one of the men questioned, as Dawson directed them to hold the Dewar flask upside down on a level with their shoulders.

'An experiment,' Dawson answered briefly, busy with the nozzle of the oxygen cylinder. 'Think yourselves lucky I'm in the scientific division. My aim is to get two parts of hydrogen and one of oxygen into this Dewar flask, in which they'll remain, if it's held upside down. I've got to guess by bulk measurement, but it ought to be near enough. After that, we need a fuse of some kind. The moment the flame gets near those combined gases, it ought to blow the steel door and maybe half the house to blazes. It's our last and only chance, before the chlorine gets too dense. Fortunately, chlorine has an affinity for both hydrogen and oxygen, so there'll be no trouble in that respect.'

The constables looked at each other and said nothing. They knew little of chemical formulae — at least, not in such a specialized way. All they could do between spells of coughing was support the flask whilst Dawson operated the nozzle of first one and then the other, directing the released gases into the inverted 'goldfish bowl'.

'Right!' he said, finally. 'That's as near as we can get it. The proportions are roughly right. Lower the flask, boys, wrong way up.'

He was obeyed. This done, he raised one edge slightly, and kept it supported by means of a sheet of paper torn from a notepad from his pocket, which he formed into a wedge. With some more of the paper, twisted into long lengths, he made a fuse that trailed erratically down the stone steps to about half way. Then he looked at the men.

'This may be our finish, boys,' he said quietly: 'The explosion will be terrific — it always is with even a small proportion of oxygen and hydrogen — and for that reason, everything may come down on top of us. Our aim and hope is that that steel door, or the wall surrounding it, will be blown away. Ready to try it?'

The constables nodded grimly.

'Right — get below, into the furthest corner of the cellar and I'll join you in a moment.'

The men wasted no time, and neither did Dawson. He flicked his lighter, applied it to the paper fuse, and then hurried down into the suffocating, odorous atmosphere as fast as he could go. Here he joined the constables, and they all crouched with their faces to the wall, waiting tensely. Such a long interval elapsed, it seemed to them that something must have gone wrong.

Then it came — ear-shattering in its violence — to the accompaniment of a blinding flash of energy as the two gases united to form water. Immediately,

Dawson went hurriedly to the steps.

'We did it!' one of the men cried behind him. 'Or rather — you did, sir!'

There was no doubt about it. The steel slide itself was still in place in its runners, the explosion not having been powerful enough to blast through it, but the surrounding wall was a crumbled ruin of dust, brick and mortar. Over everything there hung a dense cloud of smoke.

Dawson led the way out through the aperture, thankful to breathe comparatively clear air again. Reaching the hall light switch, he depressed it and, to his satisfaction, the light came up, glimmering through the ashy haze. It was also at this moment that there came a sudden commotion at the front door.

One of the constables moved quickly to open it. Instantly Harriday, Gwenda and Thompson came hurrying in.

'You all right, sir?' Harriday asked quickly.

'Just about — except for a lovely gash in the face — hello, Gwenda, still in one piece in spite of everything that's happened?'

'Like you — just about!' She gave a wan smile.

'Where's Ensdale?' Thompson demanded. 'And what's been going on in here? We heard the explosion as we came up. We came as quickly as we could.'

Dawson gave the details and then added: 'Which makes it a pretty hectic night's work for all of us. I'd better get on to the Yard immediately and have them tip off the boys to get on the hunt for Ensdale. After that, we'll get the rest of them. Oh, yes, there's an ambulance needed for 'Mopes'.'

Dawson turned and caught sight of the nearest door — the drawing room — which was slightly ajar. He moved forward, pushed open the door, and then paused in surprise. The light was presumably on from when Ensdale had left the room to track down 'Mopes'.

And, on the floor, his hands tightly clenched in a final paroxysm, was Ensdale himself.

'I'll be a — !' Dawson stopped and

gazed down on the figure for a moment, then hurried forward and made a quick examination.

'Dead?' Harriday questioned, coming in with Gwenda behind him.

'Absolutely.' Dawson frowned to himself and stood up again. 'I don't understand it. He used the antidote for snake-bite, because we watched him.'

Shelving the subject for the moment, he crossed to the nearby telephone and raised it. In a few minutes he had given his orders to the Yard; then he looked at the corpse again. Finally, he left the room and descended into the ruined basement. When he returned, he had the bottle marked 'Anti-Ser-Rat' in his hand.

'It looks to me,' he said slowly, 'as though 'Mopes' McCall was not such a bonehead as he looked. I've just made a test of this stuff below, and it's plain water. No wonder Ensdale got no result from it!'

Harriday shrugged. 'Come to think of it, that's just poetic justice in a way. He fooled the lot of you with phony mercury fulminate, so he could get the better of you and have the antidote given to him, and 'Mopes' had fooled him by turning the stuff into water. Makes you wonder where double-dealing and lying ends, sometimes.'

'I don't think it makes me wonder,' Dawson replied, putting the bottle on the desk. 'There's a corpse in the cellar, and there's one here. They speak for themselves, in a fashion. As for the rest of 'em connected with this unholy set-up, we'll find them one by one, and bring them to account. The one main tragedy, to my mind, is that a man as clever as Ensdale was, should have been so criminally-minded. If he had been entirely on our side, what couldn't he have done to make the world a lot safer for law-abiding citizens?'

THE END

CLIMATE INCORPORATED
THE FIVE MATCHBOXES
EXCEPT FOR ONE THING
BLACK MARIA, M.A.
ONE STEP TOO FAR
THE THIRTY-FIRST OF JUNE
THE FROZEN LIMIT
ONE REMAINED SEATED
THE MURDERED SCHOOLGIRL
SECRET OF THE RING
OTHER EYES WATCHING
I SPY . . .
FOOL'S PARADISE
DON'T TOUCH ME
THE FOURTH DOOR
THE SPIKED BOY
THE SLITHERERS
MAN OF TWO WORLDS
THE ATLANTIC TUNNEL
THE EMPTY COFFINS

We do hope that you have enjoyed reading this large print book.

Did you know that all of our titles are available for purchase?

We publish a wide range of high quality large print books including:
Romances, Mysteries, Classics
General Fiction
Non Fiction and Westerns

Special interest titles available in large print are:
The Little Oxford Dictionary
Music Book, Song Book
Hymn Book, Service Book

Also available from us courtesy of Oxford University Press:
Young Readers' Dictionary
(large print edition)
Young Readers' Thesaurus
(large print edition)

For further information or a free brochure, please contact us at:
Ulverscroft Large Print Books Ltd.,
The Green, Bradgate Road, Anstey,
Leicester, LE7 7FU, England.
Tel: (00 44) **0116 236 4325**
Fax: (00 44) **0116 234 0205**

Other titles in the
Linford Mystery Library:

THE ATLANTIC TUNNEL

John Russell Fearn

Deep beneath the floor of the Atlantic Ocean, scientists and engineers attempt the most daring and audacious scientific project of all time: the construction of an undersea tunnel between Great Britain and Canada; linking Land's End with Labrador. Canadian and British teams work simultaneously at either end, to converge in the middle. Using scientific methods to fight the crushing pressure and geological and marine perils involved, the brave workers face a far greater hazard — the danger within — from saboteurs!

PAY BACK

Norman Lazenby

Rick Manton and Thelma Wain were two young people in love — but they were also grifters, who recognised no moral code and considered themselves above the law. And when mobster Dan Sweder moved to take over the drug traffic in Los Angeles, they found their own small dope dealing operation was being squeezed out. Rick and Thelma had only one answer: Dan Sweder had to die! So they set out to 'eliminate' him — two small-time crooks against the Mob!

FIVE FORGOTTEN STORIES

John Hall

In the winter of 1934–1935, according to H.P. Lovecraft's *The Haunter of the Dark*, Robert Blake had settled down alone, to work ... He had painted 'nameless, unhuman monsters', and 'profoundly alien, non-terrestrial landscapes' — and also, we are told, written five short stories, later believed lost. However, an exercise book, which belonged to a certain 'Robert Blake' of Providence, has been recently acquired — the contents, when deciphered, appear to be five weird tales ...

THE LUCK MACHINE

E. C. Tubb

The world is surrounded by intangible energies of which man has little knowledge. Electricity, once an unsuspected natural force, is now a known reality . . . so why not luck? Once recognised as an actual force, the next step is to construct a machine to harness its forces. However, if one person attracts good luck, another is due for bad luck. And when the Luck Machine falls into the wrong hands, the inventors wish they'd stuck to rabbits' feet and black cats . . .